RE-VAMPING

LAS VEGAS

JEN PRETTY

The purpose of literature is to turn blood into ink.

—T.S. Elliot

ONE

"Twenty bucks!"

"I told you I won't take your bets anymore, Nia."

"Aw, come on. Chicken?"

"Broke," Ray laughed as he moved down the bar to deliver a drink.

On Saturday nights, half-drunk college kids filled the city. That's what's great about living in a small college town. The nightlife was young, beautiful and flocked to the local hot spots. Ray's nightclub was large, and the bar ran along one full wall. The opposite end was a raised DJ booth and in between was a sea of bodies writhing and churning like the ocean.

Ray's was closest to the college, and I always got in free, but Saturday night was my favourite.

My victim danced around with a drink in his hand, trying to pick up girls. Cute and soft, like a puppy, his tail flapped so fast his butt wiggled. I was sure he would strike out. The girls who came to a bar like this weren't looking for a nice boy. Wearing their low-cut tops with their hair swept up, displaying their necks like a fisherman in a market with his catch of the day.

They were dinner on legs.

Very long legs.

I downed my drink and left the barstool to join the wild party girls. They were probably going to hell, but so was I. We might as well enjoy ourselves. Music was the great equalizer, forcing us all to move to its beat in the cramped space between our bodies. The stench of sweat and antiperspirant filled the stagnant air. My sense of smell was, unfortunately, more delicate than the rest of the people in the nightclub, but the alcohol numbed it.

My teeth ached. The sight of that wiggly boy made me ravenous, but I kept losing sight of him. There he was. His sandy hair was long enough it stuck it to his forehead, slick with sweat. Then he disappeared in the crowd. I danced with the girls until I caught sight of him again. He sat at the bar, another drink in his hand. Was that his third? Hmm, college boy might be getting tipsy.

The music changed from deep bass to a sharp pop song, and the silly girls all screamed with glee.

Ugh.

I wasn't drunk enough for this. As I crossed the room, my nape prickled. A pair of eyes tracked me. Ryan. He was a moron and always had to shop at my club. There were two other nightclubs like this one in town, but Ryan still came to dinner here.

I blocked out the feeling of his eyes on my ass and slid onto the barstool beside my new puppy. I waved to Ray who shook his head when he caught sight of who I was sitting beside. He poured me another drink. Only one type of drink affected patrons like me. Ray kept it well stocked. One more reason this was my favourite nightclub.

"How are you, Nia?"

He snuck up beside me — creepy bastard.

"I'm fine, Ryan. Go away."

Ray delivered my drink. I picked up the glass and took a long sip.

Ryan didn't speak again. He stood beside me staring holes into the side of my head. I rolled my eyes and looked at him. He had coiffed his hair in a modern style. He looked like a pale GQ model with sharp teeth. Too bad he was a disgusting blood-sucking old guy and every time he opened his mouth, I heard nails on a chalkboard.

"I haven't seen you around town this week," he said, flashing me his teeth.

Like I cared about his long, pointy incisors. I wasn't a college girl, ready to throw myself at any old, gross vampire.

"That's because I have been busy and also, I've been avoiding you." I turned my back to him, hoping Ryan would take the hint and leave me alone, only to find my puppy had left.

Damn.

I turned to scan the room, but Ryan stepped in front of me, blocking my view.

"I would like to get to know you better, Nia. Is that so terrible?" He asked snidely.

God, it was fun hurting his feelings. You'd think he was a five-year-old with that pout on his face.

"Nice chat," I drained the last of my drink and left my seat. I slid through the crowd towards the restroom. Ryan wasn't likely to follow me there. I was tipsy. The 100% alcohol of the Vampire Fire hit my bloodstream, lowering my give-a-damn meter to zero. I stood next to a giggling girl at the sink and checked my makeup. The girl and her friends were discussing Ryan, of all things. Their list of his physical attributes had me stifling my laughter. Some vampires would take a human home with them, and the popular lore was that it would be the best night of their lives.

Idiots.

I smiled wide and made sure I had nothing stuck in my teeth. When my incisors flashed, the girl next to me dropped her hairbrush in the sink and turned to stare at me, eyes wide.

"Oh my god, I didn't even know there were girl vampires," she said. I turned away, satisfied that I looked lovely enough for my puppy. "Wait, can I ask you a question?"

I hissed at her, and she jumped backwards, bumping into her tall friend. The tall girl backed into the last girl in the row who was applying mascara. They were human dominoes.

Laughing as I exited the restroom, I ran right into the chest of Mr. Persistent.

"Ryan, you need to leave me alone, or we will have problems. Go find a nice human to suck on."

"Just say you will have dinner with me and I will leave you alone," he replied, giving me his creepy unblinking stare. I bet it worked on human girls.

"That is the opposite of leaving me alone."

The girls came out of the bathroom, and though the one I had scared was still looking kind of pale, they distracted Ryan, so I made my escape.

I combed the club for my puppy, stalking through the dancing bodies and scanning the dark shadows.

When I finally caught up to my target for the night, he looked dejected like someone had kicked him.

Perfect.

"Hi, my name is Nia," I said. I slid onto the barstool beside him and crossed my legs. My short skirt rode up, and I let it. His eyes lit on me and traced down my body. His face went from sad to happy in a split second.

God, he was cute.

"I'm Eric."

"Want to dance?" I asked.

"Yes!" he said with way too much enthusiasm.

Aw.

Taking his hand, I led him to a gap in the dance floor. I wrapped my arms around his shoulders, and his hands slid down to my hips. We swayed and moved to that never-ending beat. He was taller than I thought, just over six feet, but in my heels, I was 5'10" so he was the perfect height. He smelled delicious, like caramel and springtime. I pet the short locks of hair at the base of his neck. They were as soft as I had imagined.

He locked eyes with me, and I flashed him my fangs. Some people didn't like vampires, but Eric wasn't one of those people. His mouth came down on mine, and his soft lips pressed just hard enough that my fang nicked him, leaving a drop of blood behind when he pulled away.

I leaned in and licked the hot blood from his lip.

"Let's go," I whispered in his ear.

I took his hand and led him toward the back door of the club. Ray left it unlocked for me on Saturday nights. I pushed the door open and stepped into the chilly night. The rain had slowed, but it still spit drops on us as we stood in the shadows. Eric's eyes shone in the sliver of moonlight that broke through the clouds. It was still too dark to say what colour his eyes were, but I liked green eyes so imagined they were green.

I kissed his lips and pressed my body into his. He was as warm as the sun. My lips trailed a line down his jaw, and he tipped his head in invitation. I relished the victory of my hunt. My teeth throbbed in relief as they slid gently through Eric's skin, puncturing the vein hidden beneath. His tangy blood sloshed into my mouth, his heart slamming in his chest. As I drank my fill, Eric panted and squeaked. His arms held me to him like he was a drowning man and I was the only thing that could save his life. How ironic.

His body moved against mine, his hot chest sending tingles through my cold skin as his blood warmed me from the inside out.

Satiated, I licked the puncture, sealing him back up like leftovers for the refrigerator. Smoothing his sweaty hair back from his face, I smiled at him, much drunker than I had been five minutes ago and teetering on the edge of dragging him home with me.

He giggled, reminding me of the silly girls from the bathroom, and his humanity, breaking the spell. I took his hand and led him around to the front of the club where a few cabs were waiting.

"Goodnight, Eric," I said, shoving the now very sleepy puppy into the back seat and handing the cabbie twenty dollars.

Eric wiggled in the seat and gave me a crooked smile before closing his eyes. I shut the door, and the cab drove away.

Taking a deep breath of the night air, the scent of a trash fire somewhere sent me back to my earliest memory.

———

1822 Coast of Italy

Silence had fallen on our village. It had been days since my mother or father last moved. They lay quiet and still in their bed. My stomach growled when on the wind I could smell cooking meat.

I tried once more to wake my mother, but she didn't move, so I left our cottage to follow the delicious scent. The rocks and sticks stabbed at my bare feet, but I walked on until I found a small group of soldiers. They had set up a camp outside of the village with canvas hung from trees. I watched them all evening and fell asleep curled beside a poplar tree. When I awoke, they had left their tent, so I tiptoed under the canvas and snatched some dried pork and bread before hustling away.

I crept towards town with my food in my fists. The smell of cooking meat pulling me forward.

"I found two more in the cottage north of town," a man with a piece of cloth tied over his mouth said. The man was tall and muscular, like a giant. He tossed something large, wrapped in a blanket onto the fire before turning away and walking back out of the village.

I took another bite of my stolen meal and crept forward. Another masked man stood to one side of the fire, leaning against a tree. His eyes were closed, and his head rested back on the bark.

I took a few more tentative steps toward the fire. I wanted to see what was cooking in the shallow hole in the earth.

The wind shifted as I approached the edge of the fire pit and smoke burned in my eyes. I rubbed at the sting as my eyes watered, but I had to see what it was that was cooking. When the wind shifted again, I finally got a glimpse of the meat, but it wasn't pork or beef. Blackened flesh and bones littered the bottom of the pit.

I stood frozen, watching the flames lick up through a bare skull. My heart pounded in my chest and bile rose in my throat as I dropped my piece of bread.

"Hey, Thomas! You are supposed to be keepin' an eye on the fire!" The giant man with the cloth on his face said as he heaved another bundle into the fire. The blanket burned away, and I caught a glimpse of my mother's rotting face before she disappeared into flames.

I screamed, and strong arms scooped me up. I kept screaming until the man covered my mouth with his hand and blackness crept in my vision and then took over until the world drifted away.

———

Shaking the memory away, I wasn't ready to go home yet. I wished Ray had taken my bet. I'd be twenty dollars richer now.

Back inside, the night was still young and so was I. Well, I was still young for a vampire.

I danced with some visiting sports team. Maybe they were baseball players. It didn't matter. They were fit and good looking.

Ryan popped up behind me on the dance floor. He smelled like perfume and blood so was now staying in my club to irritate me. The cold chill of his body pressed into mine.

I threw my fist over my shoulder quick and hard. There was a loud crack as it hit his head. He dropped to the grimy floor, and my laughter echoed over the sound of the music, making a few humans turn our way. Ryan stood quickly, like a mannequin on strings pulled up from above and scowled at me. He muttered something under his breath and stormed away. Probably something rude. I danced a while longer before returning to the bar for one last drink.

"You gonna torment that vampire forever?" Ray asked as he set my drink down.

"I don't like vampires, Ray."

With a laugh, he replied, "You are a vampire." I touched my finger to my nose and winked at him.

The alcohol burned as it ran down my throat and into my stomach to slosh around with Eric's blood. Lost in my memory of Eric, I hardly noticed when one of the baseball guys sat beside me.

"Hey, you want to get out of here?" he asked, sitting close to my left. It was a universal pick up line. Humans had stopped using it on each other and saved it for vampires. Vampires took their cue and used it on humans when they 'came out of the casket' and the humans bared their necks to anyone with sharp pearly whites.

Bitten by a vampire — it was on everyone's bucket list.

I turned to face the cute sports guy, but he wasn't as cute as Eric. Besides, I was full and ready to get home. It was Sunday now, and I had to get some sleep before Monday morning. "No thanks, sweetie," I said, patting his cheek.

I turned back to my drink and downed it before slipping from the barstool and staggering out into the night. I was tipsy on my heels, but vampires burned off alcohol fast, and there were no drinking and driving laws that applied to us. There were few laws governing vampires. We policed our own for major violations.

So, when I started my car and aimed for home, I thought nothing of the fact I was more drunk than usual. I wove through the city streets heading to my apartment in the tallest building in the city. A full eight stories high. The street lights flashed from green to yellow, and I slowed to a stop as I neared the park in the center of town. My head was floating, as if it was no longer attached to my body. My eyelids slid shut.

A honk jolted me back to the car, and I hit the gas so hard the tires squealed. I drove on for a moment longer before my eyelids slid shut again.

TWO

"Nia wake up."

I tried to bury my head under my pillow but didn't have one, so I covered my head with my arm to block out whoever was talking.

"Nia," the male voice said again. "Move your ass, or I'll call in the Blood Guard. You know how this works."

I forced one bleary eyelid open.

Did he say Blood Guard? The dingy white of old painted cinder blocks came into focus about a foot from my face. I was lying on a hard, wooden bench, and the cold chill in the air made it clear I was not in my bed in my apartment. I rolled over and gazed in the voice's direction. As the scene came into focus, I made out the general shape and description of Officer Jenkins. He had a long face with a tiny mustache and bushy eyebrows that reminded me of Bert from Sesame Street.

"Hey, Bert. What's happening?" I asked, straightening my spine and enjoying the snaps and pops of my seized-up joints.

"You know damn well my name is not Bert. Get moving. You have an appointment with the judge." He unlocked the cell door with a clatter and swung it open on squeaky hinges. I slid off the bench I had been sleeping on and tried to straighten my clothes. My short skirt was wrinkled.

I sifted through what I could remember of the previous night. Cute Eric. I smiled at the memory of his soft hair running through my fingers.

"What are you smiling about, Nia? This is pretty deep shit you got yourself in," Jenkins chastised.

"I did nothing. I was at the club. Someone must have drugged me."

Jenkins snorted. "That's what you said last time."

OK, he had me there, but I was pretty sure someone spiked my drink this time. I should have no trouble remembering what happened last night. But everything from dancing with some muscular guys until now was suspiciously gone from my memory.

Jenkins wrapped his thick meaty hand around my arm and led me through the halls of the police station. The musky smell of dirt and stale coffee hung in the air. In the main room, there were desks set up in tidy rows with police officers in uniform at about half of them. All the officers looked away when I met their eyes, except for a young kid. Probably his first week on the job. His shoes shone in the fluorescent lights and his uniform was crisp and starched. As my eyes locked on his, I smiled, baring my fangs just a little. He sat frozen in his chair as I approached. Vampire crime training was probably pretty fresh in his mind. Most cops didn't like vampires. They thought Vampire Law allowed us too much free run of the cities, but they were too afraid to say anything to one of us. They all knew what happened when a vampire went off the rails.

It was pretty gross.

Cannibalism level of gross.

Jenkins wasn't afraid of me though. He called a spade a spade.

As we walked by the rookie, I hissed. He jumped from his seat and ran, toppling his chair in his haste.

"You really are a shit person, Nia," he said as we rounded the corner towards the courtroom.

Now that I think about it, Jenkins might have had a death wish.

"Well, it's a good thing I'm not a person then," I replied.

He shook his head and held the door to the tiny courtroom open for me. I entered and moved to the table where my lawyer, Aaron Whitmire the second, waited. His father was the first Aaron Whitmire to represent me in court. The younger Whitmire was more talented than his father and always got me off scot-free. He was worth his weight in gold.

"Jesus," the judge muttered. "Lavinia, how many times do I need to see you in a month?"

"Probably once more, at least. Third times a charm," I replied with a winning smile.

Yeah, I might have caused a small stampede at the department store on Black Friday. I told everyone in line there would be free laptops for the first ten customers. It was funny. No one got hurt. Well, no one died.

"Please, Nia?" The plaintive cry of my lawyer. He was always trying to shush me. I used my fingers to zip my lips and throw away the key.

Aaron took a deep breath. "Your Honour, could I have a moment to consult with my client?" he asked in his super-formal court voice.

The judge waved at him and took out his book of Sudoku puzzles.

Aaron sat down, and I sat beside him. "What the hell happened?" he asked.

"I have no idea. I remember nothing."

He looked at me with blinking eyes for a second. "You lying?" he asked.

Harsh.

"No, I was at the club, then I was in a cell," I replied.

"You think someone spiked you?"

Being spiked wasn't uncommon. The Dracaena plant has no taste. It only knocks us out for a couple of minutes, but some humans think it's fun to grind it up and put it in our drinks. If I catch the jerks who gave it to me, the human court system will be the least of their worries. I don't like being messed with.
Shocker.

"It fits," I replied.

"They won't believe you. You've used that excuse before."

"I remember. Thanks," I said looking around for eavesdroppers. My lawyer didn't whisper very well.

"All right, let's get this over with," he sighed. "Your Honour, we are ready to proceed."

"What did I do, anyway?" I whispered to Aaron as he straightened his tie and the judge put his puzzle book away.

"Your client is charged with driving while intoxicated and destruction of property," the judge said. "How does your client plead?"

"Destruction of property? Oh shit, is my car OK?" I asked louder than I intended too.

The judge narrowed his eyes at me.

"Not guilty, Your Honour," Aaron said, shushing me.

The judge sighed, "She is never guilty, is she? I am releasing her on the condition she wears a monitoring device and stays home until her court date one week from today. Except for one evening a week as guaranteed her by vampire law four point one when Officer Jenkins will escort her to and from an approved feeding area. Lavinia, for the love of God, stay out of trouble." With that, the judge stood and left the room.

I raised an eyebrow at my lawyer. "A monitoring device? House arrest? That's terrible work, Aaron."

"Come on, Nia. Let's get you fitted for your new ankle bracelet," Officer Jenkins said. I was still scowling at my lawyer as he pulled me away.

"I could break that hand," I said, eying Jenkins' hand as he dragged me from the courtroom.

"Yeah, yeah, but then I'd have to call in the Blood Guard, and they would call your father," he said with a bit of a sadistic smile. He loved hanging my father over my head.

Uppity human.

He walked me back through the building to the police station and into an empty interrogation room. The threat of the Blood Guard was more than enough to keep me quiet. They were ruthless vampire warriors that would hunt down their own mother and end her existence if she stepped out of line. Kind of dramatic if you asked me.

Jenkins walked out and shut the door behind him. I picked at the nail polish peeling off my fingers and waited for him to return.

A deep baritone murmur on the other side of the door pulled me into old thoughts.

———

1823 Rome

"We have a beautiful girl. Her whole village died in a plague. She was the sole survivor. The hand of God touched her."

I had heard this same speech four times already. I doubted this time would be any different. "She is quiet and doesn't cry."

The mistress who ran the orphanage scrubbed my skin that morning until it burned and dressed me in a pretty pink smock dress. She told me to keep my mouth shut and smile.

"I require an heir. A girl cannot be my heir," A man's deep voice said.

"Please, darling. A miracle girl! What a wonderful heir she would make. Let us at least meet her?"

A heavy sigh reached my ears through the closed door. "Very well, let's see her." the deep voice said.

The doorknob turned, and people entered the room. I kept my eyes on the floor, but not wanting to disappoint the mistress, I pulled back the corners of my mouth, so I was smiling.

A man's hand reached out and tipped my head up. His harsh features and dark eyes inspected me before he turned back to the mistress.

"She is small."

"She is the appropriate size for her age, but her arms and legs are very long, she will be quite refined and elegant as an adult." Mistress smiled fondly at me. It was a stark change from the way she usually looked at me.

I glanced at the woman standing behind the large man. Her eyes were nearly in tears, but she smiled at me with a tenderness I recognized from my own mother. I wanted to run to her but stayed in my place.

The man crouched in front of me and continued to study me. "Does she speak?" His sudden voice so close startled me.

"Yes, of course, she speaks," the mistress said. "She is not educated yet, but that just makes her a lump of clay, you can mould her as you choose."

The man looked back at me. "What is your name, child?" He said sternly. When he spoke, I thought I saw long pointed teeth in his mouth, but his tone demanded a reply.

"Lavinia," I whispered.

"Oh my. Lavinia means child of the King," the woman with wet eyes said as a tear rolled over her eyelid. The tear looked pink, and I wondered if she was sick, but she wiped it away.

The man stood and gazed at the crying woman for a long moment before he sighed heavily. "Very well. Come along Lavinia."

He took my small hand in his and led me from the orphanage and into my new life.

———

When Jenkins walked back through the door with the monitoring device and my purse, I remembered the judge had said something about destruction of property.

"Hey, where is my car anyway? I still don't know what I did last night."

Jenkins knelt to fit the device to my ankle. "Well, you wrapped it around the gazebo in the center of town, but now it's at the impound lot. Might need repairs," he said like he hadn't just told me that my baby was dead.

"What? My 1968 Pontiac Firebird is in the impound lot? Do you know how many kids go in there and steal stuff?"

"It's monitored 24/7, and you are lucky you didn't hit a person."

"A person is better than a gazebo! Poor Priscilla!" I exclaimed, leaning back. I'd have to get her back to the garage so my mechanic could get her back in one piece.

"You named your car Priscilla?" he shook his head like he couldn't believe he was arguing about this. "You could have killed someone," he finished with a sneer. When he furrowed his brow like that, he looked even more like Bert.

Jenkins was definitely a muppet.

"Excuse me, but I was spiked last night," I replied.

"Sure you were, Nia." He clicked the monitoring device onto my leg. It sat uncomfortably against my skin and bobbed when I moved my leg. Lovely.

"Fine, don't believe me, but get my car to Brian so he can repair it before it gets rust. Can I go home now? It will be light out soon."

Jenkins stood and held open the door then let me follow along behind him to the garage. He opened the back door of the police car; apparently, I was getting the royal treatment today. I climbed in, and he slammed the door behind me.

The drive from the police station to my apartment wasn't long. I watched the cars go by until Jenkins stopped in front of my building. He turned off the engine and got out, then held the door open for me.

"Thanks for the ride," I said.

I fished my keys out of my purse. The sun was peeking over the horizon, casting a glow across the sky. Contrary to popular belief, vampires don't have an aversion to the sun, but nothing fun happens in the daytime.

"I'm walking you up, Nia. Stay in the building, or an alarm will go off, and I will have to hunt down your vamp ass. So, stay put, all right? Some of us sleep at night."

I turned on a dime and walked through the lobby to the elevator, Jenkins hot on my heels.

On the eighth floor, I turned right and unlocked my front door.

"See ya later, Jenkins," I said slamming the door behind me. I waited until the elevator door shut and then heard the hum as it lowered Jenkins to the lobby.

I kicked off my shoes by the door and walked past the empty kitchen with the built-in island and down the hall to my bedroom. My dirty clothes went into the hamper. Sleeping on that bench had chilled me to the bone. My fingers were blue. Attractive.

My bed called to me. My heated blanket lay on top of the soft sheets and duvet, but I was icky and needed a quick warm up. The bathroom was my favourite part of the apartment. The shower was spacious with several jets that sprayed a lot of hot water.

I flicked on the shower and stepped beneath the spray. It pounded against my back in a steady rhythm. Steam filled the bathroom, blocking me away in a quiet world. I looked down at the device strapped to my ankle and wondered if it was waterproof. It wasn't electrocuting me, so it was probably fine.

When my body temperature returned to normal, I stepped out of the shower and wiped the fog from the bathroom mirror. My joints felt loose again — no more creaks. My stark reflection stared back, the same as always. So, I got dressed in some baggy sweats and dragged my heated blanket to the couch to watch my soaps.

My electric blanket kept me warm, and the constant stream of the television kept me company for the next twenty-four hours.

Monday morning arrived, and I had work to do.

I stood up and stretched. The pull of tight muscles and crack of joints felt good. I flicked off the TV and turned my attention to the laptop sitting at the kitchen table, waiting for me like a beacon in the morning light.

I started it up and then got dressed, slipped into my running shoes and walked out into the dingy hall of my apartment building. The smell of fresh paint still lingered from the walls, but the carpet was getting old and worn.

"Good morning Lavinia," a crackly old voice called.

My neighbour was about a hundred years old and human, so her face had deep lines around her mouth and at the corners of her twinkling eyes. Her hair was silver and thinning, but she kept it fluffed in a 60s beehive style. She wore monotone leisure suits and pink fluffy slippers. I wasn't sure how she still lived on her own, but she was a tough old bird, and I respected that about her.

"Good morning, Mrs. Henderson. I'm going to get the paper. Do you want one?" She could hardly see, nearly blind, but I offered to pick her up a paper every Monday for the last ten years. By now it was a tradition.

"Oh, no dear. Thank you." She reached out and patted my cheek like I wasn't twice her age. "I saw that nice gentleman walk you home the other morning. A police officer. I hope he is treating you like a lady." She rolled her walker back into her apartment.

"Thank you, Mrs. Henderson." Such a weird old lady.

I hit the button on the elevator, went out the front door and took a right. There was a variety store owned by a Muslim man named Gamil on the corner of the block. It was a tiny bodega, but it stocked my third favourite drink.

On my way in, I grabbed a newspaper and then picked up four energy drinks from the cooler. I wove between the narrow aisles until I got to the tall, crowded counter. There were all manner of things lining the counter, from lighters to candy canes to weird spinning kids' toys.

"Good morning Nia, how are you today?" Gamil said in a sing-song voice. His grey beard matched the grey of his turban today, and he looked regal and wise.

"Fine, how about you?" I asked, rooting through my wallet to find exact change.

"I am well, very well. I thank you."

He glanced past my shoulder with a worried expression. When I followed his stare, a pair of youths had come in and were staring at the drink fridge that ran along the back wall. I looked back at Gamil, and he smiled like he hadn't just had a worried look. I returned his smile and set my four drinks on the counter.

"You know those energy drinks will kill you someday," he said with a laugh.

"We can only hope," I replied, scooping up the bag of drinks and newspaper before walking back out the door.

I was halfway up the block when I heard sirens behind me and a police car pulled up to the curb.

"Damn it, Nia. I told you to stay home!" Grumpy Jenkins yelled from behind the wheel.

Oh yeah.

"I was just getting the newspaper," I smiled, holding up the offending merchandise.

"Well get your ass back to your apartment and stay there."

I gave him a salute, and he followed me in his car until I disappeared into the apartment building.

Lord, humans were hot-headed sometimes.

THREE

In my apartment, I flicked on my laptop and set out the things I needed for the next couple of days of work: four energy drinks and, of course, my heated blanket.

I unfolded the newspaper and started skimming through. There were corrupt politicians, cheating athletes, but then I found my target.

On page nine, there was a small article about a businessman named Allan Murphy. He owned several contracting businesses and a string of fast-food chains. Good old Allan was in the paper today because, over the weekend, they charged him with assaulting his fiancé. A beautiful woman named Kelly.

Kelly was a former model turned actress and Allan had taken it upon himself to rearrange her face after a loud argument at one of his restaurants. He was out on bail because, you know, he's an upstanding member of society. I bet he didn't even have a monitoring device strapped to his ankle.

I also bet this moron had a dating site profile. He seemed the type.

I opened my laptop and logged in to my private network, routing my Internet connection through a warehouse on the other side of the country. I typed a few commands to make sure the connection was secure. Once I switched to an anonymous browser, I made a hot dating profile with a picture of a large chested blond I found in an image search. Allan lived in Detroit, so I selected that city too. Sifting through the dating profiles, I found him.

He hadn't even used a fake name. Classy guy.

I sent him a little love note and then switched tabs.

I Googled his business phone number and made a quick call to his secretary.

"Murphy Contracting," The young-sounding woman said.

"Yes, hello." I used a southern accent, so I sounded more trustworthy. "My name is Nancy Shoemaker, and I am calling on behalf of my boss, Mr. Penderson." I paused for dramatic effect. "He has asked me to call you today because he's gone and lost Mr. Murphy's email address. They met at the big hoopla last month and had tucked the piece of paper with the email in his suit coat pocket, and then I accidentally sent that to the dry cleaners."

"I have been there," the woman said, and I knew I hooked her.

"This is the second time, and I'm afraid he might fire me if I can't get this straightened out."

"You would think they could do a simple thing like emptying their own pockets," she said.

I had to bite my lip to keep from laughing.

"My thoughts exactly. He would lose his head if it weren't attached to him."

The woman laughed, and I joined her.

I sighed dramatically.

"Anyway, if there is any way you could give me his personal email address, it would really help me out of some hot water."

"Sure, let me get that for you."

I pumped my fist in the air and then jotted down the address.

I thanked her and hung up while sending the phishing email that he would hopefully open, giving me access to his computer. Step one complete.

By that evening I was settling in to watch some soaps when my laptop dinged. I grabbed my mouse and woke up my laptop to find Allan himself messaged me on the dating site.

"Hey beautiful, how are you this evening?" He wrote.

"Feeling lonely, how about you?" I replied.

"Me too. I would be better if you sent me a pic," he wrote.

I replied, "I can't figure out how to send a picture here." With a sad face emoji.

"That's OK, darling. You can send it to my email." He then helpfully supplied his personal email, like a moron.

I laughed and sent him a file with two pieces of malware. One would sit in his computer and monitor every keystroke until he logged onto a bank account as long as he opened the attachment. The second one would give me access to his computer.

"Bingo!" I shouted as his computer connected to mine.

"I didn't get a picture, try sending it again," he typed into the chat window on the dating site.

I logged off thoroughly disgusted by the womanbeating bastard and happy with my success. I slipped into his files and started looking through things. He had a bunch of boring tax information, a few games and a folder called 'pix.' That looked interesting. I clicked it and wished I hadn't. It seemed our friend Allan had a bit of a fetish for large men in leather. Very small scraps of leather. The leather was covering nothing important. I clicked through a few more and was horrified to find a picture of Allan, dressed.... err, undressed in the same way as the previous men. His large gut hung forward, not quite enough to cover his man bits, though I wished it did. His breasts were nearly larger than mine, and the grin on his face was seriously disturbing.

Gross.

I popped my second energy drink and chugged it, wishing I could bleach my brain. Then I moved to my couch with my laptop to wait.

I could easily go without sleep for three or four days, but I hoped it wouldn't take that long.

I kept one eye on my laptop and watched some *Young and the Restless*. Those wacky rich people lived such dramatic lives.

As the sun came over the horizon Tuesday morning, the sound of my third energy drink can popping open was startling in the silence. Having lost all interest in TV, I played a stupid block breaking game on my phone until my laptop pinged to alert me to activity on my new friend Allan's laptop.

I dropped my phone and leaned forward, hitting a few keys until I saw what I had been waiting for. Allan had logged into his bank account, and I captured his personal account number and password. I did a happy dance on the couch cushion and used my virus to fry his laptop with enough malware he would have to burn the thing. Poor Allen. I flushed the connection to his system and logged into his bank account.

The man was loaded. He had just over a million dollars in his account. I could only imagine what the business and offshore accounts would have, but a million would do fine — a slap on the wrist.

I started the arduous task of siphoning his money into a few Go Fund Me accounts I had set up. The amount of each transaction had to be small so the bank and Go Fund Me wouldn't notice but once it was all in there, I split it between several women's shelters in Detroit area and closed up shop.

I wondered if it would make the news. Probably front page. Man beats a woman, page nine, but he loses a million dollars? That's news.

I wiped every trace of my activity from my laptop and leaned back to enjoy my last energy drink.

They didn't keep me awake.

I just liked the taste.

———

Finally, Saturday rolled around, and I was itching to get out of the apartment. Jenkins was supposed to be at my building at eight o'clock but didn't show until 8:15.

The jerk.

I slipped into the passenger seat of Jenkins' Buick LeSabre. The car smelled like old socks and fast food grease.

"Will this car even make it downtown?" I asked.

"Shut it, Nia. It's a perfectly fine car. Don't like it; you can walk."

I scoffed, but shut it, as he suggested.

Once we were downtown, I directed him to park in front of Sacred Heart Catholic Church, then slid out and climbed the steps.

"What are we doing here? You can't seriously plan to drink from someone here," Jenkins moaned. I could, if I wanted to, but I had missed confession last week, and I'd be damned if I missed it again this week.

Inside the tall chapel, the vaulted ceilings rang with the echo of my high-heeled shoes. My short dress was scandalous for a house of God, but I didn't want to have to change again before the club. Candles flickered, illuminating the stained glass and sharp stone that made up the building that was older than I was. Few things were older than me, but I could feel the history in here and see it in the wear of the wooden pews where generations of people had sat and the slight indent in the stone floor where centuries of feet had tread.

I opened the small door and sat in the confessional booth. Before I shut the door, I saw Jenkins make the sign of the cross and kneel in a pew in the front row.

Good Catholic boy.

"Forgive me Father, for I have sinned. It has been two weeks since my last confession." I whispered.

"I missed you last week, Nia. Maybe the first Sunday in 10 years. Though you know I don't expect any of my flock to come every week," Father John said.

The patterned window between us obscured his features, but I knew he had grey hair and deep laugh lines on his clean-shaven face. He was a small man, but his voice filled the church at Sunday Mass. I didn't attend Sunday Mass regularly, as mornings didn't work for my schedule, but I never missed Sunday evening confessional.

"Yes, Father, I got in a bit of trouble Saturday night. I punched Ryan, though I'm not sure that's a sin, as he deserved it."

"It is always a sin to hit someone in anger, Nia," he admonished lightly. "Is that what kept you from confession?" he asked.

"No, father, I accidentally ran my Firebird into the gazebo in the town square. Technically, I'm pretty sure someone spiked my drink, but my car is damaged. That, I know, is a sin. It took years to get the parts for that car."

Father John's soft chuckle echoed through the confessional. "If you didn't do it on purpose, it is an accident, not a sin."

Well, that was a relief. Though, if God was cool with the gazebo thing, I wasn't sure why the police were being so annoying about it.

"Though, perhaps you should make peace with Ryan. The feud between you hurts God's heart and tarnishes your journey to Him. Is there anything else?"

"I stole from a wife beater and gave the money to a bunch of women's shelters," I whispered so the policeman wouldn't hear me. Father John sighed heavily. "Nia." "I know," I replied.

He shook his head beyond the confessional window that separated us. "Say five Our Fathers and make amends with Ryan. And, Nia, no more stealing."

He said his prayer and absolved me of my sins, and I walked out of the confessional feeling light and relieved. It was nice to have someone I could talk to about anything. Father John never asked dumb questions. I knelt in the pew beside Jenkins and closed my eyes to say my prayers. Just like I did as a child.

1824 Rome, Italy

All the men and women wore their most elegant clothes. The hooves of horses pounded on the stone courtyard in front of Sant'Agata de' Goti. The church stood a million miles high to my young eyes. I was dizzy looking up at the terrifying image of St. Agatha, her breasts displayed on a plate. Her torturers removed them when she refused to denounce her faith in Christ.

We moved through the crowd as it funnelled into the beautiful building. My hand was small in my father's, his grip tight as though he worried I would run off. At six years old, I had already seen enough horrors. I stayed at my parent's sides at all times. The bells tolled, deafening me as we passed through the doors into the darkened interior. The ornate granite columns with decorative engravings stretched up arched walls that lined the nave leading to the pulpit where the Cardinal would preach to the flock that awaited him.

I slid into a bench, between my father and mother and quietly said a prayer to Saint Agatha, that I would have her determination.

———

I shook myself out of the memory, stood and left the church. Jenkins followed behind me, and we got back in his rusty car.

"To Ray's, Driver," I said, smiling at the disgruntled police officer.

"Did you snack on Father John in that confessional?"

I scoffed. "Unbelievable. I would never snack on Father John. He is a national treasure."

Jenkins raised a bushy eyebrow at me and then pulled out into light evening traffic and drove us to Ray's, where the party was just getting started.

FOUR

At Ray's, the line-up continued around the corner. I walked past Jimmy, the bouncer, and into the sea of warm, delicious bodies. Behind me, Jimmy stopped Jenkins at the door, but let him in when the officer flashed his badge.

The club was full and busy already. Ray had help behind the bar. The new bartenders made sure to serve everyone promptly. I appreciated that too. Nothing worse than waiting for a drink. The smell of alcohol wafted through the steamy air; business was good. The crowd was just a mass of limbs and bodies, no space between.

My initial excitement cooled when I spotted my least favourite type of human: Disciples. They worshiped vampires, making a whole religion out of the undead. They were mostly addicts, though. Bitten too many times and now only living for the high we could give them. It was sad and pathetic.

The black-clad group of goths all turned and looked at me, like creepy children gazing upon their hero. I turned to avoid them and got myself lost in the crowd.

"Hey, Nia!" Ray called, as I approached the bar. He smiled and poured me a drink. He liked the freaks. They were good business. But then, so was I. Nightclubs with known vampire patronage could draw business from all the smaller neighbouring towns.

"The freaks are out tonight," I shouted.

Ray laughed and gave me a double thumbs up.

Jenkins slid onto the stool beside me. "How long will this take?" He yelled.

I set my purse on the bar beside him, gave him a little wave and turned from the bar. If I could stay away from the wanna-be vamps, it would be a fun night. I wasn't opposed to having Jenkins watching me, either. Game on.

I surveyed the crowd as I danced with some sloshed girls. They were giggly and held hands; probably wouldn't make it to last call. I got lost in the music. The energy in the club was high with this many bodies, and I couldn't resist the siren call. The lights flashed and strobed as the live DJ spun records with a fast, heavy beat. As the girls moved on, I danced with a man who was older than the usual crowd; maybe early thirties. His hands roamed over my body as we moved together. His scent was delicious and made my teeth ache, but he wasn't the one I wanted tonight. Glancing back at the bar through the crowd, I saw Jenkins watching me.

I wanted him to watch.

I moved across the room, leaving the old guy behind. Clustered near the hall to the restrooms stood a group of disciples. Their black eyeliner and dark clothes gave them away. They begged for vampire attention and were always willing to be bitten, but their neediness was disgusting. I didn't want them either. They just cluttered the club.

One of them noticed me and moved through the crowd in my direction. He approached, head tipped, neck bared. When I hissed at him, he dropped to a knee. Literally. He bowed.

I threw my hands up and spun away, not in the mood for their crap tonight. I pressed past the hoard of people and back to the bar where I waved at Ray.

"Hurry up," Jenkins said. He had a glass in front of him, but I was sure it was just water.

I flipped him off. My night of hunting was turning into a bust. Ray brought me another drink, and I chugged it. Turning back to find someone to munch on, I didn't care who, anymore.

The first man I flashed my fangs at, turned away. Bastard. I wasn't about to spend all night waiting for my dinner. It was time to get home. The night-life was tiring.

The man I danced with was several inches taller than me. He had spiked hair and dark stubble on his chin. His height put him taller than I liked, but he smelled delicious, like fresh cut grass and springtime. I wrapped my arms around his shoulders and flashed my teeth at him. His eyes went wide and his muscles tensed. After a second, he tipped his head. I leaned in until my lips pressed against his skin. I licked his neck, and he drew a sharp breath. My eyes sought Jenkins at the bar and locked onto his as I bit down, piercing skin and vein beneath with the practiced aim of centuries. The man's legs gave out, but I held him up as his blood filled my body. I felt the tingle of life returning to my cold limbs, and my heart shook like an earthquake in my chest. The heat was better than any hot shower. It was like the sun rose in my stomach, covering me in its early morning rays.

The crowd around us slipped away. The sounds and lights faded until it was just me, Jenkins and the guy's heartbeat. Our rhythm was perfect. Thump. Thump.

Jenkins' eyes blinked to the same beat. The whole world in time, like constellations aligning. He watched for longer than I thought he would, his eyes trained on mine. Finally, he looked away, his cheeks pink but I could still see his fast, shallow breathing from across the club. I licked the man's neck, sealing the punctures and steadied him on his feet. I ducked through the crowd and grabbing my purse off the bar beside Jenkins.

"Let's go," I said, walking towards the door. I could feel Jenkins' eyes on me and knew he was following. I wanted to go home, have a hot shower and forget about this night. The judge had to see me tomorrow to decide what my punishment would be. Vampires had more rights than humans. We didn't have to wait so long for court dates.

I slipped into the passenger seat of Jenkins' car. He got in and pulled away from the curb.

"Do you usually just bite people in the middle of the bar?" Jenkins asked.

"No," I said and continued staring out the window as the city lights went by.

He drove in silence for a while, but I could hear his mind running through what he wanted to say. I listened to his lips part several times like he would say something, but then he closed his mouth again.

He pulled up to the front of my building, and I started to get out.

"I'll pick you up at seven tonight to see the judge."

I stepped out and shut the door then entered my apartment building and took the stairs up. Running as fast as I could, got me up eight flights in about a minute. The rush of adrenaline pushed a smile to my face, unbidden, and wiped away the last of the night's strange feelings.

Mrs. Henderson smiled at me as I approached my apartment door. Her door was wide open, and the whole floor smelled like her fresh baked cookies. I wasn't sure what kind of crazy drove a person to make cookies at two am, but it smelled great.

"Hello, Nia. Were you out with your nice gentleman caller?"

I laughed. People said I was old, but Mrs. Henderson was old fashioned. "Yes, we went to the club on Broad Street," I told her as I fished my keys out of my purse. "What are you doing up this late?"

"Oh, you know, we are having a bake sale at the church, and I wanted to make sure the cookies were as fresh as possible." She sat on her walker seat and fished a ball of yarn and some knitting needles out of her bag.

"They smell great. Good luck at the sale," I said as I opened my door and waved goodbye to the old coot.

I sat at my kitchen island and listened to the click, click of Mrs. Henderson's knitting needles until I felt chilled again. Then I tucked into bed with my heated blanket and fell asleep.

———

I woke to the sound of someone knocking on my door. The clock said it was almost six thirty. I threw back the covers and peeked through the peephole. I could see Jenkins standing in the hall talking to someone out of view. I opened the door as Mrs. Henderson handed him a box of her cookies.

"Thank you. Yes, I think Nia is special too," he said, raising an eyebrow at me.

"Ok, well I'll let you two be alone, but let me know if you need any more cookies." Mrs. Henderson turned her walker around and went back into her apartment.

Jenkins walked through my door, and I shut it behind him.

"Why does your neighbour think I'm your gentleman caller?" he asked.

I snorted a laugh and walked into the bathroom, flicking on the shower. I wasn't going to talk to the judge smelling like beer.

When I came back out, Jenkins was sitting on my couch with the remote for my TV in his hand as he surfed through all the channels.

"Do you have every channel?" he asked when he noticed me standing there watching him.

"Yeah. Can we go?" I asked.

He flicked the TV off and stood up, following me to the door, where I slipped on my business shoes, and we walked out of the building together. I had put on my light blue skirt suit that made me look reliable and trustworthy. I wore it ironically, and it wouldn't help since the judge knew me, but I should get points for effort.

The courtroom had two dozen people in it, including the women's auxiliary group that had put themselves in charge of the downtown gardens. They were like the Stepford wives: Perfect hair, perfect bodies, perfect families. Disgusting. I wanted to scare them so they peed their perfect pants, but held back hoping the judge would forget that I had caused problems before and let me go with a warning.

The women's auxiliary would cause a stink anyway, I knew it. You would think the damage to my car was punishment enough.

My lawyer stood at the table in front of the judge, and I walked down the aisle and stood beside him.

"Aaron," I said in the way of greeting.

"Hey, Nia. This should be quick."

I hummed.

"Order in the court, the Honourable Judge Barlow presiding," the bailiff called out as the judge entered the room and took his seat.

"Hello, Nia. I hear you have been mostly obeying the law this week."

The ladies muttered behind me.

"Yes, judge. Good little vampire." I used the word to remind the snitches behind me to watch their tongues. It worked. They shut it.

"Good. Listen, Nia." The judge took off his glasses and leaned forward. "The city damage to the gazebo has been repaired, but it has taken time away from the efforts of the Ladies Auxiliary. They are trying to get the town square ready for the planned Gazebo Festival. So, they have asked, and I've agreed to sentence you to 20 hours of community service to help with the gardens and clean-up of the town square."

"You can't be serious." I looked at my lawyer, but his eyes wouldn't meet mine.

"I'm quite serious. If you do not agree with my ruling, you are welcome to call in the Blood Guard to settle the dispute.

Ugh. Everyone played that card. The Blood Guard would call my father and everyone in this town knew I didn't want to see him. Maybe it was time to find a new place to live. Twenty hours, I could get that done in 2 nights. That would mean I would be a day behind for my work, but not a big deal.

Everyone in the room seemed to be holding their breath, waiting for my reply.

"Fine," I said, and they could have heard the collective sigh of relief at the edge of town.

"Excellent. I will have Officer Jenkins remove your monitoring device, and you can begin right away."

I narrowed my eyes at the smiling ladies, wiping the look right off their faces as I walked past. They would regret messing up my week.

FIVE

Finally free of the monitoring device, I took a cab home and changed into black jeans and a black t-shirt. The idiotic women of the auxiliary would meet me downtown at the gazebo to get me started on my chores. I made sure they wouldn't see me coming.

It was the dead of night as I walked back out of my building and into another cab to take me downtown. First thing in the morning I would need to call Brian and check on my car. Cabs were inconvenient.

"Town square," I said as the cab pulled away from the curb. The cabbie's eyes kept flicking to the rear-view mirror. His eyes focused on me instead of the road behind him.

"What?" I asked, after I caught him looking at me for the fourth time.

"I think I met you at the club last weekend," he said, timidly.

I looked down at his license, displayed on the back of his seat. It was my puppy, Eric.

Aw. So cute in his license photo.

I looked at the back of his head, at his soft hair and wanted to run my fingers through it again, but I knew I couldn't. I didn't drink from anyone more than once. It was a rule. Humans got weird and clingy if they stayed with a vampire too long, like the disciples.

"Sorry, you don't ring a bell," I replied blandly and turned to stare out the window until the car rolled to a stop half a block from the gazebo in the center of town. I gave him twice the fare rate and stepped out, sighing as he drove away. He smelled delicious.

In the center of town, there was a square park that surrounded a gazebo. It wasn't more than a city block. Old-growth trees dotted the area, and paved paths wandered through and led to the gazebo.

I hopped the curb onto the grass and walked into the park across the grass to stay out of the lights that illuminated the path.

Up ahead, a group of women painted the side of the recently repaired gazebo and nattered about some woman named Brenda who had an affair, but her husband didn't know. This would be fun.

They had a few floodlights set up and were buzzing away with more town pride than a Texan on the 4th of July.

They didn't notice my approach, so I stayed behind the floodlight to hide my presence until the very last second. When I reached the floodlights, I pulled the plug.

The women screamed even though there was plenty of light between the moon and the streetlight. I watched them scramble around for a minute and then walked out of the shadows.

"Hey ladies, how's it going?" I asked, strolling in as though nothing had happened.

The lights flicked back on as one woman found the unplugged extension cord and jam it back in. She was busy blaming a short, squat woman for not plugging it in properly.

"Oh, hey there," a tall thin woman said, approaching me. Her hair was taller than the statue of liberty, looking just as hard. Her yoga pants and baggy sweater screamed *mom*, and I couldn't help but snicker. These ladies would be fun.

"Hi, I'm ready to get started. Where do you want me?" I asked, smiling wide enough that my fangs showed. The supermom took a step back and then picked up a garbage bag and wooden handled trash picker. She leaned forward, her arms outstretched as far as could, trying to hand the items to me.

When I didn't take them from her, she backed up again.

"We thought it would be the easiest thing for you to do. Do you have any experience with painting?"

I tried to decide if garbage picking or painting was worse. It was a real toss-up. The garbage wasn't likely to get on my clothes, but it was still garbage.

"Give me the thing," I said, holding out my hand.

She leaned forward again, and I snatched the bag and picker away from her. I turned and strode around the gardens and manicured lawn, picking up random bits of paper and flattened soda cans.

The refuse of a material world.

They mainly used the gazebo and surrounding area for the various festivals the town planned through the year. The local teenagers enjoyed it the rest of the time. They would hang out at night and smoke cigarettes and drink cheap beer until Officer Jenkins or one of his buddies showed up to break up the fun. Sometimes I joined them. From now on they would be picking up their own damn garbage.

Once the garbage bag was full, I moseyed back to the gazebo to find a note taped to a stack of four cardboard boxes.

The note said to plant flowers from the boxes in the empty garden beside the gazebo. There was a hand drawn picture of how they wanted them planted. There must have been thousands of little flowers in the long, flat, boxes.

The top box was all white flowers. I slid it off the top of the pile and set it beside the garden. The second box had red flowers. I smiled. My favourite colour. The last two boxes had more white and red flowers. I was all set.

I got to work, digging holes in the black earth and plopping little, coloured pansies in place.

Hours passed as I worked. When I finished, I stood back and admired my masterpiece.

It was glorious.

My finest work. It would go down in history as the greatest piece of landscaping I had ever done. Admittedly it was my first attempt, but it was perfect in its genius.

The mud caked my hands and knees, and the dew had settled on the ground making me feel damp and cold all over. I moved the empty boxes into the gazebo and unplugged the floodlights, then turned and walked back towards home. I pulled out my cell phone and called a cab. I told them I was walking down the main street.

I put my cell phone away and walked the darkened streets, whistling a happy tune. The crisp autumn air filled my lungs with the scent of molding leaves and fresh bread. Up ahead, the bakery lights shone out onto the sidewalk. The baker scurried about, making morning treats for the people who worked downtown.

As I walked by the alley just beyond the bakery, I heard a noise that made me pause. It sounded too big to be a cat, and two heartbeats thumped in the darkness. I took a step out of the street light and into the shadow. My eyes adjusted to the dim moonlight as a woman came staggering out towards the street. She teetered past me, and I searched the darkness. The scent of her blood drifted to my nose, and I knew she had just been a snack.

I took two more steps into the darkened alley, my senses on high alert — a predator hunting.

A tin can rolled out from behind the dumpster at the end. I took a deep breath and caught the scent.

"You shit, get out here," I called out to the darkness.

Ryan stepped out from behind the dumpster and posed with his chin lowered and his arms out to his sides like Jesus on the cross.

"Were you trying to scare me?" I asked.

He raised his chin, displaying his wicked grin. "Just intrigue you. Did it work?"

"No, you just disgusted me," I said, walking back out to the street.

"Nia, wait, please?"

I stopped and sighed. "I'm not going out with you, Ryan."

Ryan joined me on the sidewalk, facing me with a pleading look on his face. "Let me walk you home, at least?"

The cab rolled up, saving me from the awkward and annoying conversation.

"Gotta go," I said and stepped into the backseat. I gave the cabbie my address and gave Ryan a little wave as the cab rolled away from the curb. The sun would rise soon, and the city would come back to life. Humans would rush about like ants searching for dropped candy at a fair.

Back at my apartment I turned the shower on hot to warm up and scraped the mud off my hands. It had soaked through my jeans to my knees, leaving them black and pruney too. By the time I was clean, it was lights out.

A few hours later, when I woke up, I discovered Brian had left a voice message saying he was ordering car parts. He knew I would approve whatever he had to do, so he didn't need me to hold his hand, but I wanted to check on my car, anyway.

I called yet another cab, and it delivered me to Brian's Garage just as my favourite mechanic was opening it up.

He lifted the garage door and there she was. Like a patient in the middle of surgery, the insides of my precious car spewed all over the shop floor in front of her.

"Oh, Priscilla," I exclaimed, as I stepped past Brian and ran my hand up the undamaged front panel.

"Nia, don't worry, she's gonna be fine. I'm waiting for a new radiator and then she'll just need some bodywork," Brian said in his gentle voice.

I crouched down beside my car and leaned my shoulder into her driver's side door then looked back at Brian. He was an unreasonably tall person. Probably pushing seven feet, but he hunched over, making him a few inches shorter. Most likely a habit, so he was less intimidating. I found people did that; tried to make themselves into what they thought other people wanted them to be. Brian's face was always friendly, and he was a great mechanic too, but he didn't have the drive for business, and so had been running this single-car garage his whole life.

I met Brian at a car show one summer when I was still looking for parts for Priscilla. He had a Firebird there too and helped me find what I needed. No other mechanic has touched her since.

"Thank you, Brian."

"No problem. Accidents happen."

That was true, but if I ever saw those guys I suspected spiked my drink, they might find they had an accident too.

"If the new rad comes in today, I can start body work tomorrow. Another week at most," Brian continued scratching his neck like he was nervous about telling me that.

"Take your time, Brian. I want her fixed right." I smiled, and he nodded in reply. I ran my hand over her glossy white coat one more time and walked back through the minefield of parts.

"Thanks, Brian," I said as I walked back out of the shop and headed for home. It wasn't too far to my apartment, and maybe a good walk was what I needed to get my head back in the game. I was feeling low and nostalgic which was not a good combination.

When I rounded the corner onto my street, several people were standing around outside Gamil's variety store. As I approached, I recognized a few of the people from the neighbourhood and Mrs. Henderson, my neighbour, was there too. Gamil's front door was closed, and someone had taped a note to the window.

"Oh, isn't it terrible, dear?" she said in a hushed tone as I approached.

"Isn't what terrible? What happened?" I asked, trying to read the note past her shoulder.

"I heard it was a gang." She said in a harsh whisper. "They robbed Gamil and beat him." She shook her head. "I just don't know what this world is coming to." "Terrible," I agreed.

The note said closed until further notice. I would have to get my paper somewhere else. Inconvenient.

"Do you want me to get you a paper?" I asked Mrs. Henderson.

She studied me for a moment then slowly replied: "No, thank you, dear." Like she wasn't sure if I was serious.

I carried on down the street past my apartment building. Another block farther there was a newsstand. They didn't have energy drinks, but they had newspapers.

I bought one and walked home. The sun was getting up in the sky, and I was getting cold again.

Back in my apartment, I flicked on my laptop and heated blankets. Time to get to work.

The front page was a story about a man named Ed Florence. They had arrested Eddy boy in connection with some bad street-drugs that were killing people. He was released because the only witness in the case turned up floating in a river. Also, Ed was a vampire. The Blood Guard was investigating, but so far had found no link between Ed and the floater.

I went to work on our new friend Ed. Criminals were harder to steal from because they knew first-hand about stealing and were paranoid beyond belief.

I traced an email address through the website of a nightclub he owned and sent him an email saying I had blackmail photos of him and that he needed to drop one million into a dumpster behind a street in his city I picked randomly. The attachment was the real prize. When he opened it, I would have remote access to his computer, but he would see a picture of a kitten in a birthday hat.

I moved to the couch to wait. Setting my Laptop on the coffee table, I wished I had some energy drinks, but it was too late now.

About an hour into my wait, there was a knock at my door.

I opened it to find Jenkins standing there, his arms crossed and bushy eyebrows raised to his hairline.

I smiled. "Good morning Officer. What can I do for you?" I kept my body in the doorway. I didn't need him inside while I was working.

"You want to explain yourself?" he asked.

"I have no idea what you mean,' I replied, hand on my chest, ready to swear innocence.

"I was just downtown. The Women's Auxiliary called me, in hysterics, because someone made an anarchy symbol out of flowers in the centerpiece garden bed that was supposed to have the town name in it."

I couldn't hold it in anymore. I laughed until tears, of bright red blood, rolled down my face.

"You better fix it tonight, or the judge will hear about it, Nia."

I took deep breaths to calm my laughter so I could speak. It took a few more minutes. Jenkins tapped his foot and waited. He had no sense of humour.

"Ok, fine. Tell them not to get their panties in a bunch."

He scowled at me, then turned on his heel and stomped off. The poor, long-suffering police officer, lowered to settling disputes about flower arrangements. I laughed several more times over the next few hours remembering Jenkins' eyebrows.

SIX

The rest of the day was a bust. Either Ed didn't check his email very often, or it had gone into his junk folder, and I would have to try a different tactic. It was getting dark, so I showered again and changed into some clothes I didn't mind getting dirty. Fixing my flower garden would suck; I thought it was top notch work.

I took a cab downtown and had it drop me off at the gazebo.

The lady with the tall hair who had introduced herself last time and whose name I had forgotten, was there with the other grumpy-looking ladies.

"Oh, hey there, Nia. So, I guess, uhm, if you don't mind doing the flower garden, we will be over here raking the leaves." She must have lost a bet, or maybe she was at the bottom of the pecking order in this group of old hens. She was even more nervous tonight than last night.

I smiled at her, licking my fangs. She stood frozen like a deer in headlights. She stood there staring at me for so long it got super awkward, so I turned around and got to work.

The town name, Belcrest, looked fine in the flowers. Not as nice as my original art, but I suppose these people had zero taste for these things. I should have taken a picture of my original art.

"Nia," I heard from behind me as I was planting the last row of white flowers. I recognized the voice, so I kept working. My luck could be worse, probably.

I felt Ryan come up and stand behind me and didn't like how close he was. I wished I was swinging a hammer so I could 'accidentally' let it go of it and nail him in the nuts. But alas, my only weapon was a floppy pansy, and that was a pretty pathetic weapon.

I planted the final flower and stood, dusting off my hands. I turned around reminding myself what Father John had said. "Make amends". I was struggling to remember why I had cared about personal growth in the first place when the idiot vampire was breathing down my neck like I was the last bit of blood on earth and he hadn't eaten in a month.

He smelled like blood and vanilla. Some silly girl had already donated to the mouth breathing Neanderthal earlier in the night. He most likely feasted every evening, despite how unnecessary it was.

"What do you want Ryan?"

"I want to see you. I heard a rumour you were here, digging in the dirt like a commoner."

"Ryan, oh my god, you can't just call people commoners," I said in my best Mean Girls voice. He gave me a quizzical look, apparently not up to date on pop culture. "How old are you? Get with the century, Ryan."

"I changed my name just 50 years ago," he complained. Like changing his name qualified him as current. Most vampires fell into the same trap as Ryan. Outdated and weird. The silly girls that worshipped the old vampires thought it was charming.

Barf.

"Ok, well, I have work to do."

"You wouldn't have to do this if you had simply called your father," he muttered.

I spun around and glared at him. He flinched, which made me smile on the inside. "I do not need to call my father. You leave him out of this or I will cut out your tongue!" Ok, so sometimes when I get angry, I speak in an old-fashioned way too. The threat was real though, and Ryan raised his hands, palms forward in a placating gesture.

He followed me back to the gazebo, where the ladies were packing up to go home. It was well past midnight, and I wondered if they had been sticking around to keep an eye on me and their precious flower garden.

"Oh, hey, thank you, Nia. That looks so great. Listen, we are going home, but if you could finish bagging the leaves, that would be just so wonderful." The woman's eyes kept darting between Ryan and me. Her cheeks were a bit pink, and I wondered if Ryan had snacked on her at some point. Probably had. He was a blood slut. I wasn't sure there were any women left in the town he hadn't snacked on.

"Sure," I replied, grabbing some paper bags off the steps on the gazebo and walking out towards the first pile of leaves.

Ryan didn't leave. He watched me struggle with the stupid paper bag for a while then came over and took it from me. He held it open, and I scooped up leaves and squished them in. I was pretty sure there was dog poop in the leaves and hoped some of it would smear on Ryan. He was wearing an expensive t-shirt. One of those top designer labels that cost two hundred dollars in the store but made by some poor kid in a sweatshop for pennies.

Ryan didn't speak while we worked. Thank god. His voice was smooth and fake and always irritated me. When I packed the last of the leaves into the last brown paper bag, Ryan spoke.

"Come to dinner with me tomorrow night," he said.

"I don't eat till Saturday night," I replied, setting the bag of leaves with the others. "I'll pick you up at 7."

I looked up at him. His smug smile screamed: caught you!

I flipped him off and headed out of the park.

"Come on. Please, Nia! Just once!" He called from behind me.

I stopped and turned back. He had been pretty helpful with the leaves.

"Fine, 7 pm. Just once."

His teeth flashed in the moonlight before he turned and walked out of the park.

I plucked my cell phone out of my pocket and called a cab. Hopefully, Ed had checked his email. I needed to get some work done.

————

Back in my apartment, I showered and changed into comfy clothes. I woke up my laptop to find my buddy Ed had opened my attachment and sent a reply filled with threats of violence. I used an encrypted email address that he wouldn't be able to trace, so I wasn't worried about his rant. Some of his suggestions were physically impossible anyway.

I logged into the software setup to trace my malware through Ed's system. He had some high-end firewalls, but I snuck through and his computer linked up to mine giving me remote access to his network. I downloaded the keylogger software and flicked on my TV to wait. My fingers and toes were still cold, so I curled up under my heated blanket and waited for the upload to finish.

After a particularly startling pregnancy reveal on the soap opera I was watching, my laptop pinged letting me know the keylogger was up and running.

Now I had to wait for my new friend Ed to log onto his bank account, and I would be golden.

Waiting around was boring. He wasn't using his computer. So, I checked the remote access software to see if he had a webcam. He did, so I took a peek.

I expected to find an empty room. Instead, what his laptop camera captured was Ed, his arms around a woman with long blond hair and Ed's teeth sunk deep into her neck. Ed was not a tidy drinker. Blood ran down the woman's naked back as Ed's eyes flashed in the low light of the room. I watched, shocked for a few minutes. He kept drinking, and I wanted to tell him to stop as the woman's arms flailed weakly and stopped moving entirely.

He dropped her lifeless form to the floor with a hollow thump and sucked in a deep breath. I could practically see his heart beating with the blood he had consumed, but draining a human was against the law. The Blood Guard would kill him for this — no trial. Ed was dead meat.

Ed's eyes fell on the laptop. There shouldn't have been any signal I was using the camera, but Ed yelled, and a few other vampires came into the frame.

"Get Donnie in here and find out who is using my computer!" he yelled, then he pointed at the camera. "I will kill you, you hear me? You are dead!"

I shut my laptop so fast it almost fell off the table. I sat there staring at it for a minute like it was a bomb about to go off. Then I gave myself a mental kick, and I opened it again. I needed to cover my tracks. If he had a talented hacker, he could trace my connection. He shouldn't have known I was even in there.

I deleted my malware and then wiped my hard drive and closed my laptop again. I sat there staring at it for a few more minutes. That wasn't good enough. I stood up and tucked my laptop under my arm as I marched to the basement, set it inside the trash compactor and hit the button. There was a loud crunch, and it was gone.

No one had caught me before. Not even close. Nobody even suspected me of Internet crimes. I had gotten lazy and reckless. That wouldn't happen again.

I took the stairs back to my apartment, burning off the bit of adrenaline I still felt. Then I locked my door and the windows, just for good measure. I scolded myself for being paranoid. There was no way his hacker could find me now. I tucked into sleep for a couple of hours.

At sundown, I took a cab to the mall. There was a high-end electronics store owned by a local guy named Darren. He could hack, I was sure. He was the only person to suspect I was up to no good with my laptop. I replaced mine more often than average, but my continued patronage assured his silence.

My father thought he could buy me back by padding my bank account. He couldn't, but he was rich, so I spent his money, and new laptops were my main purchase.

The mall was overrun with teenagers and old people pushing wheeled walkers with bags full of knitting supplies or whatever. No sensible person went to the mall when they could help it. The long wide hall with escalators down the center made way for the shops and department stores where well-dressed women and men rang through purchases of clothing and electronics. Beautiful women at cosmetic counters sprayed passersby with perfumes that smelled like toilet cleaner. The teenagers hung around in a group like a cackle of hyenas, laughing raucously and shoving each other.

"Hey, Nia," Darren greeted me as I walked up to the counter. He was geeky, in a cute way. His glasses made him look smart and his shirt and tie- professional. I had seen him in the club a couple of times though. Not a complete nerd.

"Hey, Darren. How's it going?"

"Not too bad. What can I get for you today?"

"Something fast and pretty," I smiled. He knew I didn't tinker. I wanted a laptop ready to go, like usual.

He smiled and went into the back room.

I waited at the counter and watched a kid read the backs of all the video game packages by the front of the store. The kid was no more than thirteen years old and kind of motley. He wore an over-sized coat and his hair was shaggy and unkempt. He looked around and then tucked one game into his coat. I almost laughed but bit my lip. There was a security tag on everything in the store. Cue the fireworks.

Just as Darren came out from the back carrying my new toy, the kid walked out between the alarm sensors and lights and sirens went nuts.

"Hang on a sec, Nia," Darren said as he went storming off after the kid. I walked to the doorway and watched as the kid raced down the hall towards the mall exit, Darren in hot pursuit. Mall security nabbed the kid before he made it out the door and he started screaming like a stuck pig. I laughed and watched as the kid squirmed trying to break free of the overweight security guard.

Once the guard had the kid well in hand, he told Darren he would call the police, but Darren just took his game back and told the kid not to enter his store ever again--probably scared him straight. Or set him up to be a career criminal. Either way, everyone settled down, and Darren came back to ring me through.

"Sorry about that, Nia. This has been happening more and more. I'm thinking about putting the games behind a glass case."

"You're pretty fast. I thought for sure that kid would make it."

Darren looked at me and raised an eyebrow. When I didn't respond, he chuckled and rang through my purchase. "You're a strange one, Nia. I hope this laptop lasts longer than the last one." He put it in a bag, I thanked him and walked back out of the mall.

SEVEN

The rest of the night I spent on the couch, loading up my new laptop with the software needed for my work. One failure couldn't get me down. I needed to push forward and try again next week. With the laptop set up, I tucked into bed to catch up on sleep.

A solid twenty-four hours later, the sound of my phone ringing woke me.

I slid my hand across my coffee table, knocking off empty cans with a clatter until my fingers slid across my cell phone. "Yeah?" I mumbled into the phone.

"I'm a bit early. Can I come up?"

"Who is this?" I asked, rubbing the sleep out of my eyes.

After a pause. "Ryan."

"Why would I let you come up?" I asked, before remembering earlier in the week. "I'll be down in a minute." I did not want that sleaze in my apartment, but I had said I would go out with him. He better be taking me somewhere fun.

I showered and got dressed in a short, off-the shoulder dress, realizing I would need to do some laundry soon. Or maybe stop at the mall again and buy new clothes. Laundry day sucked.

My hair pulled up into a messy bun, I took the elevator to the lobby. I found Ryan leaning against the mailboxes, chatting with one of the young women who lived in the building. She laughed a bit too loud at whatever funny thing he said, putting her hand on his chest and flipping her hair. Little tramp.

Ryan straightened when he saw me. Leaving the human standing there alone, he took my hand, placing it under his arm and resting my palm on his forearm. Very old-fashioned.

"I have the perfect place for dinner," he said, leading me past the gawking woman and out to his car. He drove a black Bugatti. It was a new car, but at least it was fast and had guts. I'd have thought less of him if he drove something that had no go. I still much preferred American Muscle.

He drove out of town and got onto the freeway.

"Where are we going?" I asked

"It's a surprise," he said. His pearly white teeth reflected in the oncoming traffic headlights.

We drove in silence until he pulled off the freeway into the city.

"Please tell me you aren't taking me to Club Black."

"No, everyone knows you hate the little goth kids. It's public knowledge, Nia."

He pulled up in front of a high-end nightclub with valet parking. I admit I rarely got into the city and had never been to this club. I wasn't even sure it was vampire-friendly. Not that it wouldn't be fun to crash a non-vamp club.

Humans couldn't keep us out, but we were just more likely to get a meal in a place they expected us to be. Dinner was dinner, but we still liked to hunt when we felt like it.

Ryan left the engine running and got out. He opened my door and offered me his hand. I rolled my eyes but accepted his help out of the low sports car, and he linked my arm with his again, leading me to the front door of the club. The music was loud for an upscale club, but I soon found out why; it was full of rich kids. They were the eccentric spoiled offspring of the bigwigs of Hollywood, and judges and whatnot. It was a sea of skin. The hot club encouraged a 'less is more' approach to clothing. What clothes they wore probably cost as much as my rent. They were the beautiful peacocks of the human world. Delicious.

We stopped at the bar. Ryan waved, and the bartender smiled at him before abandoning the other people she was serving, to serve us.

"Hey, Ry," the woman shouted over the music.

"Monica. This is Nia," Ryan said.

"Hi, nice to meet you. Can I get you each a drink?"

"Thanks," Ryan replied, and Monica scurried off.

"You come here often?" I asked.

"Once a week. These kids here are in full rebellion, and it suits them to have a vampire in the club."

I laughed. Rich kids always had to push the envelope. I didn't mind, more fun for me. The music only got louder as the night slipped by. Ryan and I danced and drank and hunted. Ryan kept looking at a redhead. Wild curls bounced around her face as she danced to the music. Even in the low light, I could see the spatter of freckles across her high cheek bones. I tried to decide between a punk kid with a mohawk and a jock with arms as thick as my waist.

Ryan moved in and whispered in my ear. "Go for the punk. He looks fun." I guess I hadn't been subtle.

"All right, go get your ginger," I said, pushing him away. He laughed and lurched off through the crowd in pursuit of his exotic Irish lass.

I made my way towards the DJ booth where I had last seen my little rocker boy but he was gone. I moved around the dance floor and back to the bar, but I couldn't see his mohawk anywhere. Disappointed I went to the washroom to check my make-up. Inside, girls snorted coke on the bathroom counter. They were laughing and falling to the floor. This place was wilder than Ray's or any of the other clubs at home.

Back out on the dance floor, I found Ryan, and he smelled coppery. I was still hungry and bummed about losing track of my punk. I looked around for a new target, but Ryan spun me around by the shoulders and gave me a little shove. I realized he had found my guy. I slid up next to my prey and snaked my arm around his waist. He looked down at me and smiled. He wrapped an arm over my shoulders and danced with me. His body moved like liquid, and in the flashing strobe lights of the club, I caught his chocolate brown eyes.

I flashed him my teeth, and he leaned down and kissed me. Humans sometimes still surprised me. My punk boy had a tongue piercing. He licked my lips, the warm steel ball tracing the line of my mouth and I opened for him. He tasted like bourbon, and when he broke away, I slid my mouth down his coarse stubbled jaw to his neck. His hand slid up to tangle in my hair as I bit down, and my senses exploded on the rich taste of him. He continued to move against me to the beat of the music, rolling his head back in ecstasy. When my heart beat once hard in my chest, I sealed up his wound and kept dancing with him for a while longer. He had drunk little alcohol, and I didn't drink much of his blood, so he was still quite functional. He was a good dancer, and his body was warm.

Eventually, Ryan cut in, and I said goodbye to my hot punk boy with the tongue piercing.

Ryan's hands roamed my body and I let him. I was a little blood-drunk and it was nice to dance with someone I could take home if I wanted.

Ryan pulled me from the dance floor and bought me another drink. I downed it fast to keep the relaxed feeling from fading. Then he swept me up again and I forgot all of the reasons I shouldn't let him get too close.

His hand ran up my arm and across my bare shoulder to wrap around the back of my neck. He pulled me close and I felt his breath brush my collar bone. I wanted to tip my head back and let him bite me. I wanted to feel that exquisite pain and pleasure, but I wasn't that drunk. I spun out of his arms and danced with a group of girls until the last of my alcohol burned off and it was pushing towards closing time.

Ryan tossed his arm over my shoulder as we walked out into the crisp, damp air.

My ears rang in the silence outside after so long in the loud club. Even our shoes on the sidewalk sounded strange. The valet brought Ryan's car up, and he opened the passenger door, settling me in before he tipped the valet and got behind the wheel. The car engine roared through the nearly empty streets of the city as Ryan took us back towards the freeway.

"It wasn't so bad, was it?"

"What's that?" I asked

"Going out with me?"

"I suppose not. The club was nice."

"And the company?" he asked, eyes on the road.

"Acceptable."

Ryan smiled and drove on in silence for a few minutes.

As he pulled the car off the freeway and through the streets of our little city, he glanced at me a few times.

"What is it?" I asked, getting annoyed by his eyes flashing in the moonlight.

"It's just," he glanced at me again. "We would be a good pair, Nia. I'm old enough to lead a coven, and your father would give you any city…"

"Shut your mouth, Ryan!" I scowled. "Is that the only reason you wanted to go out with me? So, you can get your coven?"

"Not entirely. You are hot as hell, Nia. I want my city. I've waited long enough."

"So you thought you could speed up the process by taking me out for a good time? God, you are all alike." Thankfully he pulled up to my apartment building, so before the car had even fully stopped, I threw the door open and got out. Then I slammed the door, making the window rattle and cutting off whatever Ryan was saying. He couldn't just leave it alone though, so he got out too.

"Nia, come on. You won't want to live in this shit hole forever. You should consider your future." His voice had taken on a whining tone that reminded me why I hated him.

"Shut up, you self-important turnip!"

I scurried into the building, shutting the security door behind me so he couldn't get in unless he wanted to break something or wait for someone else to let him in. Then I took the stairs up to my apartment as fast as I could run and locked myself in.

Stupid vampire hierarchy. Everyone always jockeying for position and trying to get to the top. This was exactly why I stayed away from them. Idiots.

I slid down to sit on the tiles by the door. I was still warm from the club and the blood, but the memory of my last moment as a human chilled me to the core.

———

July 20th, 1837

My presentation party was a huge celebration. All of my nineteen years, father kept me away from society. I was excited to have so many of my father's colleagues present for my big day. Father said I was an adult and would take my place at his side. His heir. Not that he had a throne, but he insisted that soon he would be king and I would be a princess.

My mother twisted my hair into tight curls and mounded them atop my head. The dress she chose for me was pure white. The skirt and train, beautifully gathered and embroidered in a gold thread at the bottom hem. The material was light and fine and suited my slight figure. The short sleeves puffed, making my arms look more slender by comparison and the white of the fabric complimented my olive complexion.

Mother wrapped a shawl over my shoulders and smiled at me. I caught sight of my reflection in the basin and I couldn't believe how mature I looked. Finally grown.

Mother walked me down the stairs of our home to the soft clapping of the men and women in the parlour. Father looked proud, his chest puffed up and accepting the congratulations of the other men.

I knew, even then, that most of the men were vampires. Mother and Father raised me with the knowledge and it was simply a fact of life. Glad to have pleased my father and impress his friends, my smile was so wide it hurt my cheeks. Father bore my inability to act as he expected with so much patience.

"Thank you all for coming today," my father spoke. "I am overjoyed to present to you today, my heir, Lavinia."

The crowd clapped respectfully.

My father held out his hand towards me and I moved to step forward, but my mother stopped me with a quick hug before she dropped her eyes and hurried out of the room. I followed her with my eyes and wanted to chase after her, but my father's voice stopped me.

"Lavinia, come stand with me," he said in his authoritative voice.

I knew not to disobey my father, he had taught that lesson well, so I did as he commanded and walked towards him. His hand still extended in my direction, I placed my small hand in his and he pulled me to his side.

"On this joyous day, we welcome Lavinia to our family. We make official what has been in the making these 19 years. Her beauty is beyond compare and her intelligence will make her a most valued asset to any household."

A chill ran up my spine. I felt like a horse at auction in the market. He listed more of my attributes and education. I pushed down the sick feeling. The smile on his face as he gazed upon me was the best feeling in the world. He never looked at me as though I were more than a nuisance. I didn't truly understand what would happen to me that night.

Many of my school friends had spoken excitedly of their presentation parties where being formally presented to society was a big moment in their lives. They said how wonderful it was to attend parties and meet interesting people. I had lived a quiet life, spending all my time on my studies. We hadn't travelled or met many people and the idea thrilled me.

Music began to play and father took my hand and danced with me around the room. He spun, and I soon became dizzy, smiling and laughing. Father even gave me one of his rare smiles. The night was perfect, and I hoped perhaps now I would please him, and wouldn't upset him so often.

The rest of the vampires began to dance. Some danced with humans who had come in as the music began. Others drank wine and toasted my father.

When the music finally stopped, I was panting and my legs shook from the vigorous dancing, but my father wrapped me in his arms and held me tight.

I clung to his strong arm and giggled until his teeth broke the skin of my neck. I screamed, but then my body went limp. I tried to raise my hand, but it was as though it was no longer under my control. My mind was dizzy as though I was still spinning around the dance floor. His teeth retracted, but he didn't pull away from me. I had seen him feeding once before when I crept downstairs at night, but this was different. He continued to drink my blood until I felt sick from the spinning.

I tried to push him away, but I was so weak. I kicked my feet until my slippers fell off and my legs stopped obeying my command. Finally, my vision went blurry and tunneled down. My eyes found my mother's face. She stood by the back wall. Her hand over her mouth and bloody tears running from her eyes. I didn't understand why she wasn't saving me. I was dying. My heart slowed, my eyes drifted shut, the last of my blood drained from my body, and then there was nothing but blackness.

———

I sighed and considered staying on the floor but heard soft feet on the carpet outside my door. Too light to be human. It was probably Ryan coming back to try to weasel his way next to my father again.

I sighed and pushed myself off the ground, ready to tell him to get lost when my door, the frame included, came crashing into my apartment, barely missing me.

I jumped back as a wooden stake whizzed past my head. It sunk deep into the drywall, raining dust down on me and shocking me into motion.

A masked man entered through the ruined door as I dove behind the kitchen island. Panic clenched my muscles. I had nothing to defend myself with. I spun, wishing I had a steak knife or heavy pot. Another stake sailed past my head and embedded deep in the cupboard. No human could throw that hard. Now I knew it was a vampire. I grabbed the stake, pulling it out of the cupboard door. I threw it back at the masked vampire.

He dodged behind the wall, then came forward again, pulling his arm back to throw another stake. I grabbed the only thing I had in the kitchen, an electric kettle, and threw it. It hit him in the head knocking his aim off. His next stake missed me, but he recovered quickly and threw another. This one sunk into my arm making me scream. I pulled the stake from my arm, releasing a gush of blood and threw it back. It hit him in the stomach. He yelled and turned, running out of the apartment.

I scrambled up and sprinted to my bedroom, locking the door behind me. My phone was on the nightstand.

I hit a button and waited, my hand wrapped firmly around my still oozing wound.

EIGHT

"Yeah," Jenkins' sleepy voice came over the line.

"Jenkins, a guy just tried to kill me."

"What?" he sounded more awake now.

"Some guy just broke down my door and tried to stake me in my apartment," I yelled.

"Jesus, Nia. Where are you now?" I could hear sheets rustle.

"In my bedroom," I replied, looking around for another weapon. I had nothing. "I staked him in the stomach, and he took off, but I can't find anything to use as a weapon."

"Go across the hall to Mrs. Henderson's," he said.

"What if he is still out there?"

"Go, Nia!" Jenkins' stern voice got my feet moving. I hung up the phone and tucked it in my pocket.

I unlocked the flimsy bedroom door and peeked out. It was silent. I crept back through my apartment and pulled a stake out of the wall. Then stepped onto my flattened door and peeked out the hallway. There wasn't anyone there. I tiptoed across the hall and raised my hand to Mrs. Henderson's door but before I got the chance to knock, her door swung open. I screamed and then she screamed and clutched her chest.

"Nia, you scared me. What are you—" she noticed my kicked-in door and as her old eyes flashed back to me, squinted at the blood on my sleeve. "Come in here."

I walked into her apartment, and she locked the door behind us.

"Here, dear." She ushered me to her kitchen table and unwrapped a plate of cookies. "Have a cookie."

"You know I can't eat them, but they smell delicious."

"Oh, that's right. I always forget you people don't eat."

I laughed at her use of the term 'you people'. She was such a sweet old lady.

"What happened to you?" she asked, sitting across from me at the small Formica table.

"Someone tried to kill me," I said, fiddling with the stake in my hands.

"Oh, my! I don't know what this world is coming to. Who would want to kill you? Such a sweet young lady." She nattered on for a while longer about back in her day. Thankfully a knock at the door and Jenkins' voice calling from the hall interrupted her. I jumped up and walked to the door before Mrs. Henderson could get herself up from her chair.

"You ok?" he asked, his eyes tracing over me until he saw the blood on my arm. He grabbed my hand and pulled my sleeve back, but the skin had knit back together already. Still hurt though so his rough handling made me hiss at him.

He raised a bushy eyebrow. I wanted to laugh at the thick caterpillar on his face, but I was figuring out what had just happened and who was responsible. I couldn't find any humour in the situation.

"Come on. The Blood Guard is on its way. They had a team a couple of hours away so we'll leave your apartment for now and you can come down to the station." Two police officers were standing at the door to my apartment.

"Ok," I said. I turned and thanked Mrs. Henderson, who gave Jenkins a plate of cookies, and then I followed him down to the police car outside.

"Someone tried to kill you?" He asked when we were in his car and driving through the city.

"So it would appear."

"You know why someone might want you dead?"

I paused. I wasn't sure how much to tell him, or if I could hide any of it from him. If I kept quiet, I would have to go home. I couldn't live on my own.

"Nia, this is deeper shit than you have ever been in. Your father is already on his way. There is no point lying."

"Fine, God, Jenkins. I was just on the internet and accidentally saw a video of someone killing someone else."

"A video?"

"A live cam."

"And who was this person?" he asked.

"Ed Florence."

The car swerved. A horn blared. Jenkins straightened back into his lane, and visibly collected himself.
He took several slow breaths.

"You are in a lot of trouble."

"Yeah, I got that, thanks," I said impatiently.

"Ok," he said taking a deep breath. "Let's just wait for the Blood Guard."

He pulled the car into the garage at the police station and killed the engine. We got out and walked through the station to an interrogation room. My nose burned with the smell of vomit and urine. I sat down in the cold chair.

"You need anything?" Jenkins asked.

"No, I'm fine," I lied, as I set my head down on the table and closed my eyes. I had put in a lot of time and effort keeping away from my father. One stupid mistake and now I was back within his grasp and probably going to end up floating, face down, in a river.

Jenkins left me alone for a few hours. I gave up sulking and played games on my phone for a while. I was about to log into my on-line TV account when Jenkins returned.

He wasn't alone.

"Lavinia," my father said in his uptight, proper kingly voice.

"Father," I replied in a mocking tone.

He scowled at my tone. "What mess have you gotten yourself into?"

"Nothing I can't handle. You didn't need to come."

"Yes, well…" My mother cut him off when she came bustling in. She nearly had a cow when she saw the dried blood on my sleeve.

"What happened? Oh, my poor baby!" she cried.

I rolled my eyes. 200 years old, but still her baby. "I'm fine momma. It was just a cut."

"They said someone tried to stake you!" she smoothed my hair back and put her hand on my cheek. Her eyes darted around my features. Trying to find other injuries, but there were none.

"Well, they didn't succeed," I replied shortly.

"Lavinia, do not speak to your mother in that tone."

Here we go.

Momma turned on my father, pointing her finger at him. "She nearly died! Go talk to your Blood Guard and let me have one moment of peace with our daughter before you chase her off again!"

It had been ten years since I'd seen my mother, but I had never heard her stick up for me before. Or talk back to my father, for that matter. Some things change, I suppose.

My father turned on his heel and walked back out the door. Jenkins followed, leaving me alone with my mother.

"I'm sorry, momma."

"It's ok, darling." She knelt on the floor in front of me and wrapped her arms around me. I hugged her back. She was warm and smelled like candy and home. I missed her for the first time in a decade. What's a decade when you live centuries or millennium?

I grew up with the finest of things, attended the most expensive schools and wore the finest clothes. I always had enough to eat and they guarded me against the illnesses that killed most children of the time. The best thing, though, was my mother. She spent every waking moment with me and sometimes slept with me at night. Her gentle love was the counterbalance to my father's strict, controlling nature.

"I can't come home," I whispered into my mother's hair.

"I know," she said, but her voice caught at the end. We embraced each other in the interrogation room for several more moments. I knew she was crying, but she covered it well, and when she let me go, she wiped her face on a silk handkerchief from her purse before she looked back at me.

Her candy scent clung to my shirt the way I wanted to cling to her. She was my safe harbour and I felt like I was a child again when she was near.

"I love you, momma."

"I love you too, sweet Nia." She brushed my hair back from my face, and we both took deep, steadying breaths. Then I laughed at the irony of us. What a pair.

"You need to go somewhere safe. Please, Nia?"

The door opened, and Jenkins walked back in with a harassed look on his face. My father had that effect on people.

"Your father wants you to go home-"

"No," I cut in.

"I figured you would say that, so witness protection and the Blood Guard have come up with a coven that can keep you safe."

"It would have to be a major city coven, to keep her safe," My mother said, looking suspicious. "What city are you speaking of?"

"Las Vegas."

My mother pursed her lips and nodded slowly like she didn't want to admit it was a good place. I hadn't met the coven leader of Las Vegas and probably didn't want to if he was powerful enough to protect me.

"Can't the Blood Guard just go kill Ed and I can get back to my life?" I moaned.

"You know how this works, Nia. You are the only person who witnessed this murder. Without proof of a crime, the Blood Guard can't act."

"As if I'm not a reliable witness," I muttered.

Jenkins' eyebrows went up into his hairline.

"Fine, whatever, Bert," I sneered.

He narrowed his eyes at me but said no more. I counted it as a win.

"All right, well, your father left. If you are ready to go, we can leave for Vegas now."

"Fine, let's stop by my house so I can pack. I better stop at Brian's and tell him where I'm going too."

"You can't do that Nia. Nobody outside of witness protection, Blood Guard, your family and myself will know where you are. We can't risk anyone else. Buy new things in Vegas. I'm sure Mr. Merewin will help you out."

"I have my own money," I said.

"Not anymore, Nia. You can't use your bank accounts or even use your name. You will have time to pick a new one on the way."

"I like Nia!"

"Tough," Jenkins said. "You shouldn't have been messing around with evil murderous vampires. I told you that someday all of your crap would catch up with you."

"Ok, Mr. High Horse! I get it! Let's go then." I moved toward the door.

"Nia," my mother's soft voice brought my attention back to the room. She walked over and wrapped me up in a hug again. Her strong arms pushed my broken pieces back together for a moment before she let me go and I shattered once more.

She didn't say another word, just disappeared out the doorway. I took a deep breath and let my mind settle, then waved Jenkins on, and he walked me back down to the garage where we got in a plain car with tinted windows, and he drove us out of the city in silence.

Las Vegas was across the country — 12 hours of endless highways and several rest stops. I didn't understand why humans drank so much coffee if it meant they had to stop every few hours to urinate. Apparently, it's a touchy subject as it caused Jenkins to scowl so hard his eyebrows nearly touched when I brought it up. I kept the heat blasting to stay warm, though Jenkins complained. I counted the beads of sweat that ran down his forehead to disappear in his eyebrows like they were 2 super absorbent sponges until he yelled at me to stop staring at him.

As the scenery slipped past, I fell into a memory of travelling with my mother and father.

———

France 1880

"Lavinia, while we are in the city, you must behave like a proper lady. I won't have you running about the market making me look like a fool." My father's stern voice echoed through the carriage.

"Yes, father," I said solemnly before turning my eyes back to the passing hills lined with vineyards. Their perfect rows mocked the landscape which fought to shake them off as it rose and fell in steep green hills.

We often travelled once I was a vampire. We had been visiting a wealthy family of vampires who lived in a castle near Paris, but father felt the political atmosphere in the country at the time was getting too close to violence and wanted to stay clear of it.

Also, it was getting colder and being locked indoors through another winter would be torturous.

We had been travelling by carriage for five days, switching horses and drivers at small towns along the route so we could continue without stopping. The villages and long stretches of bumpy roadway offered little in the way of diversion. I was pleased to be finally nearing Montpellier. The bustling city was near the Mediterranean Sea where we would take a boat south for the winter months.

As the sun rose, neat rows of grape vines traced the hillsides that led to the city. I could feel the pulse of a city nearby and as we traversed the last hill the city lay before me like a beacon. Its white stone buildings with beautifully carved facades called humans from all around to buy and sell and trade. The church spire rose in the center like God himself had reached down and formed the peak from heaven above.

The clothing of that time was uncomfortably restrictive. Tight corsets and wide skirts were in fashion. They were excessively elaborate, and father deemed we must look like the height of royalty.

Father wore a coat and breeches. They were the finest materials, but still infinitely more comfortable than what popular fashion forced me to wear. Mother never complained, always smiling and seeming the perfect royal wife.

When our carriage finally stopped on that Sunday morning in front of the church, the bells tolled and everyone from the streets and surrounding communities filed into the ostentatious place of worship to hear the bishop speak and pray for their wretched souls.

My legs had nearly seized, but I walked from the carriage to the church doors, humbly behind my father, his tall hat perched regally on his head. His presence caused other men to move aside and make way. Mother and I were caught up in his wake as he strode to the front of the church and sat in the first pew, where another group of vampires waited, leaving space for us.

I sat beside a female vampire dressed in similar fashion to me. She fidgeted uncomfortably, and I felt a kinship to her as the bishop had us rise for the opening hymn. The man waxed on about sin and deliverance, his monotone voice barely changing in pitch. Later, the church pew creaked beneath me when I shifted, but a scathing look from father sufficed to still me. The girl beside me caught my eye and winked mischievously. I decided she was perfect and hoped we were seated together because we would stay in their home while in Montpellier.

After the final hymn was sung, and the Bishop released us from our stained glass prison, I followed behind father. He spoke in French to another expensively dressed vampire.

"I will have my driver follow you through the city, Lord Mackreth," He said.

"Superb, I have a party planned for this evening, I hope you will not be too weary from your travels," Lord Mackreth replied.

"We welcome a party after such a long time in the carriage. Thank you." My father could be gracious. I saw it when he spoke to other men. Particularly those who could bolster his political ambitions.

When I saw the woman who sat beside me in the church step into the carriage with Lord Mackreth, I smiled, knowing she would be there. Five days in a carriage with my father was too much. I needed better companionship. A young vampire like myself was the perfect remedy.

I watched the city go by out my window. The narrow streets gave way to the tall, imposing arched aqueduct. The horse's shod hooves echoed on the stone as I peered out over the city and finally caught sight of the small lake of water diverted from the St. Clement spring. It was a marvel of construction. Bringing water from 14 km away, into the heart of the city. Humans would go to such great lengths to stay alive for such a fleeting moment. Their lives but a blink of time.

Our carriage pulled up to a castle-sized home. The female vampire I sat next to in church came bounding out of the first carriage smiling as if she hadn't a care in the world. She raced over and grabbed my hands.

"Lavinia, right?" She spoke in French.

She took my hand in hers and pulled me back into the castle as my father's stern gaze warned me to behave.

"My name is Cosette. I have only been a vampire for a year and have been waiting for you to come since my Lord got word of your planned visit. We will have so much fun tonight at the ball. Hurry, we have to get ready!"

I laughed. It was still before noon, but Cosette's enthusiasm was contagious. We spent the day together talking about men and clothes and hairstyles. All the most critical topics for spoiled wealthy vampires. The Ladies maids did our hair and tied us into our dresses.

We ran down the stairs giggling and holding hands. The large main floor was set up for the party. There were tables set with apples and cherries and wine glasses, filled to the brim. Dozens of vampires scattered about, but

Cosette and I huddled together giggling at the tight breeches the men wore.

Cosette was turned into a vampire because she was pretty and vampires of the time enjoyed pretty things. We still enjoy pretty things, but there are more laws now about changing humans into vampires. The coven had taken her in when the vampire who turned her died during an ill-fated attempt on the life of the coven leader, Lord Mackreth.

One of the handsome vampire men we had giggled about, came over to speak to us.

"Hello," he said bowing regally.

"Hello," we repeated.

"Would you lovely women like to accompany me on a walk through the gardens?" he asked, holding out his hand.

Cosette and I agreed, and he led us through the door to the rose garden. Its fragrant blossoms scented the cool night air. We stopped in the center, and I tipped my head back to gaze upon the stars. Cosette and the handsome man were chatting animatedly about something or another. I considered the universe, standing there in the starlit garden. The earth and the moon were in perfect harmony as they spun through the dark sky like lovers in an endless dance.

"You are so beautiful," the man whispered, suddenly in front of me. I tore my gaze from the stars, and he peeled back his lips in a silent hiss, displaying his fangs. It was against the laws for a vampire to feed on another, but I was becoming as rebellious as France, so I tipped my head. One of his arms wrapped around my waist and another around the back of my neck as he held me in place. I caught Cosette's longing gaze over his shoulder and beckoned her forward.

As I had hoped, she came to us and rose to her toes so she could reach the man's neck. I watched her dainty, white teeth sink into his skin as his fangs pierced mine. The euphoria washed over me, weakening my knees. It was short-lived though.

"What's this!" My father's harsh voice cut through the night like a knife.

A guard ripped away the vampire who had been drinking from my neck. More guards filled the area, stomping on the blooming roses. The coven leader stood behind my father.

"Is this how your household runs?" he demanded of the Lord Mackreth. The Lord's accusing eyes bore into mine, though I knew he wouldn't speak out against my father.

"It most certainly is not." The vampire Lord waved at one of the guards and pointed to the man. The guard then staked him, with no mercy. The air rushed out of my lungs.

"Father! That isn't necessary!"

"It most certainly is! These two attacked you!" He yelled though I was quite sure he knew the truth. No vampire stands still and lets someone drink their blood.

"Please, Father." A scream cut the night air, and before I could stop him, another guard had staked Cosette. Her scream cut short as she collapsed to the ground. Her face, that had been full of joy and life, was now slack and empty.

Dead.

"That is the punishment to fit that crime," my father said, staring into my eyes. A warning. Not my first, nor my last, but one of the most memorable.

———

I shook the memory away and stuck to thoughts of the present for the rest of the trip.

NINE

Finally, Jenkins drove into the city that never sleeps. It was an oasis for vampires. Most of my kind dined every night. I found no value in dining more than once a week, but gluttony wasn't solely a human trait.

Jenkins pulled up to a modern hotel-casino called Red Oasis. The outside lights were all red, giving the building an atmospheric glow. There was a steady flow of people going in and out the front doors; they all looked happy and eager to throw their money away. The sheer volume of people startled me after the last decade in a small city.

Jenkins stopped at the curb, and we both got out. He gave his key to the valet, and we entered the casino through one of several revolving doors. Inside, the sounds of coins clinking and electronic beeping filled the room with an atmosphere of wealth and high class. The humans lined up at slot machines and huddled around green, felt-covered tables, cheering and drinking. There were no windows once you walked through the revolving doors and into the casino. It was lit with a red filter, making it seem like sunset.

"Hello, you can follow me," said a vampire dressed in a suit with a com in his ear. He was big and burly, obviously security.

Jenkins and I followed the man through a door into a corridor that wound around the casino floor, and then he took us up and escalator and to a door with the nameplate "Mr. Merewin" on it.

He knocked once and opened the door.

"She has arrived, sir," said the security guard before ushering us in and closing the door behind us.

"Hello, Officer Jenkins," The vampire behind the desk said as he stood and walked around the desk, his arm extended to shake Jenkins' hand.

"Yes, good to meet you Mr. Merewin. Thank you for the escort. We would not have found you tucked away back here. You have a beautiful casino." Jenkins was gushing. Weirdo.

"Thank you, please call me Matthew," he said before his pale eyes turned my way. "You must be King Garth's daughter. I'm happy to have you here," he held out his hand for me to shake but I just looked at it. Of course, he would refer to me that way. The old boys club didn't change.

He dropped his hand. "What name are you going by?" he asked, pretending I hadn't snubbed him in front of a human witness. He had game. I'd give him that. "She decided on Ren in the car," Jenkins supplied, helpfully.

"Ren it is. Welcome to the Red Oasis. I have a few rules. One— do not dine in my casino, tired people can't spend money. Two—you must show up on time for your shifts. Three…"

I stopped listening. He had a bunch of rules and droned on forever. When he finally stopped talking, I didn't reply. I had been coming up with fun ways to break his first two rules instead.

"Does she speak?" he asked Jenkins.

"Yes, I speak. When I find someone worth talking to, Matthew."

"Nia, be nice."

"You mean Ren. Perhaps I should go by King Garth's daughter for the rest of my life. That might save us all the trouble of remembering I am separate from him."

"I apologize, I didn't intend to offend you," Matthew said, smoothing out his tie.

"Whatever," I muttered. "I don't work. I make my own money."

"Ren, whatever you were doing before is off limits," Jenkins said. "You can't do anything to bring attention to yourself. Besides, I assume it was less than legal."

"So, I'm supposed to work all the time? I might as well be a slave," I said.

"Our employees only work forty hours a week, Ren. The shifts are negotiable. If you would like to work forty hours over two days or six hours a day, every day, I can arrange it. In return, I cover your housing and small pay for necessities."

"I have nothing. Just the clothes on my back." Jenkins had bought me an oversized shirt at a truck stop in Texas, so I wasn't walking around in my bloody shirt anymore.

"I have set up an account for you at our boutique shop. Officer Jenkins informed me you would arrive with nothing. If you require anything else, you can simply let me know."

I stared at him. I couldn't explain why I needed a high-end laptop, so I didn't ask. I would have to find another way.

He wanted something from me. He was being nice. I hated that I didn't know what he wanted. This fake nice crap would not get him whatever it was he thought it would get him. Or whatever.

"Very well, perhaps you would like to see your room and get settled. I have you booked to train with Carson in the morning, but if you would like to dine and rest between now and then, that would be advisable."

"I don't eat till Saturday."

He looked stunned for a moment and then straightened himself out and nodded. "Very well."

He hit a button on his desk, and the burly security guard who had led us in opened the door and Jenkins and I followed him out. He took us down another corridor to a lobby and then we took the elevator all the way up. On the top floor, everything was quiet.

"Only vampires on this floor," the security guard said then led us to a door at the end of the hall. He scanned a card on the door and pushed it open before handing me the card. I pocketed it and walked into the room. It was a typical hotel room but had plush living space and a separate bedroom. The living room had an overstuffed couch and chairs in front of a big screen TV which hung on the wall. It was the siren call of my people. Vamps and TV, it was a thing.

Blood red vertical blinds were bracketing the floor to ceiling window that looked out over the city. The lights flashed outside the window like a giant pinball machine.

"Thanks," I said to the security guard as he turned and left.

"Well, Ren, what do you think of your new digs?" Jenkins asked from behind me.

I peeked into the bedroom. A King size bed sat in the middle of the room, and another door to one side I assumed was the bathroom.

"It's fine," I said, flopping onto the couch.

"All right, well, the force has booked me a room here for the night, but I am whipped, so I'm going to go check in. I leave in the morning. If you need anything between now and then, give me a shout."

I nodded, and he walked out. I wondered if that was the last time I would see him. Humans were fragile.

I woke up so cold I couldn't bend my arms or legs. Pushing off the couch, I staggered like a zombie to the bathroom where I turned the shower tap to hot. I struggled to get out of my clothes and stepped under the scalding water to wait for my body to heat up again. It took nearly half an hour before I could bend my knees.

In that time, I had formulated a plan. There were hackers in every city. I would have to find one and get some work done when I wasn't working for stuffy

Matthew. Matty, definitely Matty. I smiled to myself and got out of the shower. Putting my dirty clothes back on, I walked out of my new suite, pocketing my key card, and wandered down to the casino lobby.

The lobby itself sat adjacent to the casino, but you had to walk through the casino to get out of the building. On the other side of the lobby was a string of shops. From clothing to electronics to a pharmacy. You could live in this hotel and never leave. I assumed that was the point.

The casino was brimming with people. Old ladies sitting at slot machines, young guys huddled around card tables. The tinkling music of the games combined with the flashing lights to turn the room into a wonderland. I roamed around checking it all out until the security guard from the day before walked up.

"Follow me," he said, his face a stern mask.

"Ok," I replied laughing. I had no idea where he was taking me, but I followed anyway.

He led me back through the same halls as last time. The corridors echoed with our shoes on the cement floor. As we went up the escalator this time a line of men with briefcases handcuffed to their wrists came down the other side. I stared open-mouthed. If they were full of money that was a lot of money.

The security guard just kept walking as we got to the top of the escalator. I followed behind until we arrived at Matthew's door.

He knocked, then opened the door and waved me in, closing it behind me again.

Inside it was more dimly lit this time than last, and Matthew was behind his desk, scribbling away on some papers.

I took the opportunity to look around. His floor to ceiling bookshelves had everything from novels to encyclopedia. Certificates and diplomas from various Ivy league schools decorated the walls. Law, business, medicine. Matthew was well and thoroughly educated.

"Find anything that interests you?" He asked, still looking at his papers.

"Why did you take so many fields of study?" I asked, inspecting his Harvard Law diploma to see if it was real. I would know, I had one the same with my name on it.

"Because I enjoy many things," he said.

I rolled my eyes.

"I wanted to talk to you about my expectations."

"You already gave me your rules," I said.

"Yes, but I don't think you follow the rules. In fact, I bet you have already planned which rule to break first." I hadn't, but only because I couldn't decide.

He smiled, and a dimple appeared on his left cheek. Oof. That was cute.

"Ren, I only want you to fit in here."

"Why would you want that?"

He studied me for a second, and I looked back at the wall, uncomfortable with the assessing way he was looking at me. My eyes fell on a psychiatry diploma. I hoped he wasn't trying to analyze me. Freaking psychobabble.

"You are part of my coven now."

I snorted. I didn't belong here. Hopefully, the Blood Guard would take care of Eddy soon, and I could go home. In the meantime, I had to pray Brian wouldn't sell my car to pay for the parts. I was sure he wouldn't. He was a stand-up guy. Probably.

Matthew sighed. "The ladies are waiting for you in the shop. They have your uniform for work but you can also pick out some things to try on so you can change out of that shirt."

I was still wearing the Texas shirt. It had the state of Texas drawn with a mouth full of sharp teeth, eating the word Texas. The shirt had grown on me. It was all I had left of my last life.

"You can take those clothes to the laundry if you want to keep them."

It was like he was reading my mind now and I was pretty uncomfortable. Luckily there was a knock at the door. A pretty, blond vampire sashayed up to Matthew's desk in her short skirt and high heels. She set down some papers, bending at the waist, so she nearly popped out of her shirt. I laughed, turning back to the bookcase.

"Thank you, Stacy. Have you met Ren?"

Stacy looked me up and down with a fake smile on her fake face and then curled one side of her lip up. She popped out one hip and held her hand out for me to shake.

"Nice to meet you," she said.

I raised an eyebrow at her but kept my arms crossed, looking her in the eye. It became a stand-off. Finally, I looked past her shoulder to Matthew.

"Thank you, Stacy. That will be all."

She scowled at me then turned on her heel and smiled sweetly at Matthew. Oh, the poor stupid bimbo.

Once she left, I turned back to the bookcase and pretended to read the novel spines.

"Are you always so anti-social?"

I turned back to look at him, and he was leaning back in his chair, his hands behind his head. His dress shirt stretched across his chest showed a hint of the muscle he was hiding underneath.

"Are you shrinking me?"

"How would you feel if I said yes?"

I flipped him the bird and went back to studying his book collection. He chuckled.

There was another knock on the door.

"Saved by the floor manager," he said. A man walked in. He would have to have been in his late 50s when he became a vampire. "Ren, this is Carson. He runs the casino floor and trains the new employees. He is your go-to guy for everything work-related." "Good to meet you," I said.

"Nice to meet you too. You ready to learn to deal cards?" he asked, clapping his hands.

"Ok," I said.

"Great, I'll show you the basics, and you can practice for a while before your shift," he said, turning back towards the door. He opened the door and stepped out.

I waited.

He popped his head back in. "You coming?"

I walked after him without giving Matthew a second glance.

———

"So, have you ever dealt cards before, Ren?" Carson asked as we walked back down the halls.

"No, I like making bets though." I remembered all the bets I had taken from Ray. He was a fun human.

"Well, you will take bets, but also, deal cards. There is a specific way you have to deal them, by the end of your first shift you will be a pro."

He led me into a room covered in TV monitors, and six vampires were sitting in reclining chairs, watching the monitors.

"I couldn't have this job?" I asked.

"The boss thought you might like to be closer to the action."

True, I would most likely get bored sitting here all day.

"So, this is what you will be doing." Carson pointed to one screen. The woman behind the table was sliding cards out of a box and turning them over in front of people. "It's called blackjack. The goal is to get a sum of twenty-one or as close as possible without going over. It's a pretty simple game and the most popular." "All right, sounds fun," I said sarcastically.

Carson pulled a deck of cards out of his pocket and sat down at a table in the corner of the room. I sat across from him, and he did a fancy shuffle then dealt me two cards. One face down, one face up and dealt himself the same.

"Now what?" I asked.

"Now, you look at your face-down card and figure out how many points you have. If it's a face card, it's worth ten points and if it's a number card, it is worth the number shown. An ace is worth one or eleven whichever will get you as close as possible to twentyone."

He dealt me about a dozen hands, and I started winning, so he said I had the hang of it and handed me the deck. Then he brought out a strange looking machine.

"This is a continuous shuffle machine. It shuffles the decks and prevents cheating." He took the deck of cards from my hand and placed it in the machine. It made a slight sound and then a card peeked out of the slot on the front. Carson slid his finger down the card and slid it across the table. He did the same with another but turned it face up.

"Cool."

He smiled and motioned to a monitor. "I'd like you to sit with Jay and watch the blackjack dealers for a while until you think you have the pattern of hand movements down. If you stray from the pattern, one of these guys will send an alert and security will show up at your table to check things out."

I moved to sit where he indicated and saw at least fifteen cameras were watching various angles on the tables. Several of the cameras were watching a close up of the dealer's hands.

"Is that in case the dealer steals or cheats?" I asked.

"Yeah, it's surprising how often the employees try to steal," Jay replied, his eyes never leaving the monitors.

"Good, I will see you later for your first shift, Ren."

I waved bye to Carson and sat down beside Jay. There was no sound on the monitors, so the room was silent once Carson left.

I rubbed my arms and legs, the air conditioning in the room was pretty high.

"Why are you cold? You forget to eat?" Jay asked, eyes still trained on the monitors.

"No," I replied. My interest in learning something new had vanished. Time to go. I walked out of the room and I roamed the halls for several minutes before I found a human and asked for directions to the lobby.

TEN

I stepped inside the boutique clothing store and found a hoard of beautiful women dressed in expensive high fashion with hair to match. Made up plastic dolls. The heels of one woman clicked in my direction as I checked the price tag on a pair of pants. Ridiculous.

"Can I help you?" the woman's voice oozed with disdain. It was probably my Texas t-shirt. It was visually offensive. I hissed at the Barbie doll, and she almost toppled off her six-inch heels. I chuckled and stuck out my hand for her to shake.

"My name is Ren, you have a uniform for me, and I need clothes too." Matthew had money. I could spend his money.

"Of course," the woman said, reaching out gingerly to take my offered hand in a quick shake.

"So, Deb," I said, looking at her name tag. "I don't like froo froo type clothes. I need jeans and t-shirts and at least one all black outfit. Plus something slutty." I looked her up and down. "Like what you are wearing. You can gather me some things to try on while I wait.

Off you go." I sat in a chair by the dressing rooms and played games on my phone while Deb scurried around.

She came back with some nice things that fit well, and I felt more like myself as I walked out of the change room in skinny jeans and a pale blue t-shirt that fit snuggly and didn't have a caricature on the front. I slipped into some cute heels that made me tall enough to be intimidating to other women and walked back out, leaving my dirty clothes for Deb.

"Thanks, I'll wear these out. Can you have the rest delivered to my room?"

"Sure. Thank you, Ren," Deb called from behind me as I walked out of the store.

I walked through the luxurious hotel lobby, and past a coffee shop as a young man stepped out. I bumped into him, but he didn't seem to notice. He was young, maybe eighteen, but he was scrawny like he hadn't grown into his body yet or wasn't eating enough. Tucked under his arm was a laptop and he clutched it as he jogged to the door. The laptop was not cheap. I would have thought he stole it except it had stickers all over it.

I stood and watched as he continued out. He was either a gamer or a hacker. The coffee shop he had come from had a sign advertising wi-fi. I knew it was fast too because I had connected to it when I was playing my games in the clothing store.

I would have to keep an eye out for the kid.

At the end of the hall, I walked onto the casino floor and found the bar with a long line of bar stools. It was early in the evening, but time seemed inconsequential in here. Every time I had come in, it was like the evening. Like maybe 9:30 on a Saturday night. My favourite time. I was starting to enjoy the lights and siren sounds of the machines. It was as if vampires belonged in this place.

"What can I get for you, honey?" an older woman behind the bar asked.

"Sorry, I don't have any money," I said.

"I'll cover her tab," a voice said from behind me.

I turned around to find a tall, muscular vampire giving me a cocky half grin.

"No, thanks," I replied, turning my back to him.

"Aw, come on honey, It's just a drink."

I sighed and rubbed my eyebrow, feeling a headache coming on. Males vampires did that to me.

He swaggered up to the bar stool beside me and hooked one leg over it, so he was still standing but was hovering over me, his crotch in my personal space. Disgusting. I slid one bar stool over and flipped him off, but, persistent bastard that he was, he just followed me.

"Look, I don't want to cause trouble, so you need to go aim your fangs at someone else."

The bartender had wandered off to serve someone else, leaving him and me to fight about who would and wouldn't pay for any possible drinks she would pour for us.

"I just want to buy you a drink. I'm quite wealthy," he said, flashing me his yellowed fangs again. God, that's so pathetic.

I flashed him my fangs, and apparently he hadn't been paying attention when I said no before because he suddenly found somewhere else to be. I turned my attention back to the bar and realized someone had sat down on the stool on the other side of me.

"Boss asked me to tell you, he is covering your bar tab until you get paid," the security guard said. Well, that explained why the vamp had run off.

"Ok," I said.

The guard stood and strode off again. I started to feel like big brother was watching. Looking up, I saw the small camera behind the glass dome, right above the bar. I waved. Someone was watching me. I would have to remember that.

I ordered a drink the next time the bartender came past and sipped it while watching the people in the casino.

It wasn't like the nightclub; there were people of all ages and descriptions. All of them looked happy.

After a few drinks, I went up to my room and changed into the uniform. Someone had delivered it, along with the rest of the clothes I'd selected and hung everything in the closet. That was handy.

A few minutes before my shift, Carson found me and led me to a green felt-covered table.

"You will stay here. This is usually a quieter table because it's so far back, but you should have some people and I'll send a regular your way if he shows up. He likes breaking in the new people."

"Sounds painful," I said sarcastically, and I turned my attention to the card shuffling machine. Carson laughed and walked away. Sink or swim, I guess.

I stood at the table for half an hour before anyone came over. A bald man with a pot belly plopped his chips down on the table, and I dealt out the cards. He quickly lost and left without ever saying a word.

I chewed my fingernail and tapped my toes. Standing around here was the most boring thing I had ever done. In my whole life. Two hundred years. Never. This. Bored.

Also, I was getting damn cold. I started shifting my feet, trying to keep my legs moving. A group of giggly women came and sat at my table. One of them had a shirt that read 'Bride,' and the rest all had matching shirts that said 'Bride's Tribe.' They were all pretty tipsy but very enthusiastic.

They were amusing, trying to figure out how to bet and play the game. I dealt the cards and tried to keep from laughing at their antics. They lost every hand, and I had a ton of their chips when they finally staggered off towards the bar. I couldn't bend my knees though, and my arm movements were awkward and choppy. The security guard stopped by my table and watched as I dealt out a few hands to an old couple. When the old folks left, he asked me to follow him. Another woman, wearing the same uniform as me took my place.

My shift wasn't over.

Uh-oh.

I gracelessly walked through the casino floor towards the door that led to the back hall. He was marching along as usual, but I was creaky and stiff and moved much slower. He noticed I wasn't behind him and stopped to wait for me. When I caught up, he turned and walked more slowly until we were in the back hall, then he turned on me, pulling the earpiece out of his ear.

"Why haven't you eaten?" He said in an accusing tone.

"Because, nosy, I eat on Saturdays. I'm just cold. It's like sixty-five degrees in there."

"If you had eaten, you wouldn't be cold," he scoffed before turning and walking to the boss's office in silence. I wanted to have a hot shower, or maybe the hotel had a sauna. I would kill for a sauna.

He knocked on Matthew's door and pushed it open, then shut it behind me with a bit more force than necessary.

"Ren, how was your first shift?" he asked, but I was pretty sure it was a rhetorical question, so I didn't answer. "You only lasted for 3 hours."

This time he didn't ask a question, so I didn't have to answer him.

He rubbed his face with his palms and leaned back in his chair. "Can you tell me why you only dine once a week?"

The tone of his voice changed. This was the same tone he used last time when I was pretty sure he was trying to figure me out — his psychiatrist's voice.

I smiled, flashing my teeth at him. "Keeps my teeth white," I said with a lisp.

I watched him struggle not to laugh. "This is going to be a problem. If you can't stay warm enough to work, how will you work?"

"I don't work."

"Correction, you didn't used to work. Now your life has changed, and you need to do this small amount of work in exchange for my protection. That is why you are here, remember?"

I narrowed my eyes at him. There it was. He didn't need to rub my nose in it.

"Fine, I will eat more often."

"Before each shift."

"Twice a week."

He looked like he wanted to continue to argue. "Fine, now that we have that settled, you did well otherwise. I would ask you not to scare the ladies in the boutique though. Deb was quite unsettled."

"Deb was rude. I didn't appreciate her tone."

"Ok." Matthew rubbed his forehead like he was put out. "Please, try not to scare people. If you have a problem with someone, talk to Carson or me or Thor."

"Who is Thor?"

"The head of security. He led you here," he replied, shuffling papers on his desk.

"His name is Thor?" I asked with a laugh.

"Do not mock him." He pointed a finger at me.

"Ok, Matty, I won't mock him," I couldn't control the giggles though.

"Matthew," he corrected.

"Right." I turned and walked back out of the room. Closing the door behind me, I caught sight of the scowl on Matthew's face and laughed my way down the hall.

After a few wrong turns, I made it back to the lobby where the elevators were, I went up to my suite and took a hot shower.

Carson had left a message saying my next shift was in 12 hours, so I grabbed the swimsuit I had bought at the boutique shop and went back down to the lobby to find a hot tub or a sauna. I was sure there would be both; a place like this wouldn't skimp on things like that.

The man at the front desk directed me to the lower level, and I found what I had been looking for.

The sauna was huge and had a dozen people in it. It was steamier than I preferred. I liked a dry heat more which was why my heated blanket was so perfect, but heat was heat. I sat on the hard, wooden bench and leaned back listening to the surrounding conversations.

A small group of older men were here on business. They discussed market projections loudly for about twenty minutes, but hushed when a tall, beautiful woman walked out, then they discussed her assets for a while: men, all the same.

After an hour I finally felt warm, and I went back to my suite to watch some soaps until I had to get back to work.

An hour before my shift, I dressed in a cute, low-cut top and some tight skinny jeans. The top was short enough that I flashed some skin when I raised my arms. Perfect for the club. I wouldn't have a ton of time, but I could hunt a bit and have a snack before work. That should satisfy my bossy boss. I was walking through the lobby when I spotted a truly beautiful man. He was tall, with a rough beard that made him look like a lumberjack.

Usually, I didn't like a man with a beard, but this man's eyes were so green, they nearly glowed. Green eyes were so rare — emeralds in a sea of sapphires. Instead of continuing to the nightclub down the street, I stood and watched this man check in at the front desk. He had a bag in his hand and took a key card from the front desk clerk. I followed him to the elevator where he stood waiting for a car, checking his phone. I stood just behind him. Close enough to get his scent in my nose, but not to get his attention. He smelled like musky cologne and rain on a hot day. I relished it, and my teeth ached. The elevator stopped on a higher floor and my impatience made me twitchy. I wanted to take him somewhere private and bite him.

He tucked his phone away as the elevator made a soft bing and then he stepped on, and I stepped on behind him. I brushed past him and felt the heat of his arm through his shirt.

"Sorry," I whispered, as I stood beside him.

"No worries," he said, smiling.

I flashed my teeth at him, but he looked away before he noticed.

"Are you staying here?" I asked.

"Yes, for the weekend."

"You want to come up to my room?"

He looked back at me, and I smiled again. This time he saw my teeth, and I heard his heart kick up a notch.

His blood was just beneath the surface. I could see the small bulge pumping in his neck.

"Are you a vampire?" he asked, with a slight accent.

His voice shocked me out of my new love affair with his jugular vein.

"Yes, never met one before?"

"I'm from Canada," he replied.

That explained it. It's so cold up north. Only a few vampires went there, and only in summer months. No vampire in his right mind would live where the snow flies.

"Let's go to your room," I said. If he passed out, I didn't want him in my bed.

He nodded as the elevator doors slid open. I walked close beside him, and he found his room. He let us in and set his bag on the bed. His room was much smaller than mine — A bed on one side and a TV on the other.

"What do I do?" he asked.

I took his shaking hand and wrapped it around my waist. I put my hand on his jaw and I tipped his head to the side. His Adam's apple bobbed nervously. I ran my fingers through his coarse beard. The whiskers gave way to soft skin at the bottom of his neck where it met his collarbone. I leaned in until my body was against his. I licked his neck low by his collarbone. The soft skin there smelled delicious. He shivered. Goosebumps rose on his arms, and his fingers flexed on my hip. His breathing sped until I thought he might hyperventilate. It had been known to happen. I took it as a compliment. I slid my teeth into his neck and he sucked in a quick breath, his body tensing before he relaxed into my arms. He was soft and pliant now. Boneless. His head lolled to the side as I drank from him.

The door behind me opened, I turned with a hiss, gripping my prey like a greedy lion on the Serengeti.

"That's enough, Ren. Come with me," Matthew said.

I licked the puncture, my eyes locked on Matthew's and then used every ounce of my strength to let go of my lumberjack. He was my prize, my prey. I had won him fair and square. I reminded myself I wasn't an animal and slowly let go of the man. His beautiful green eyes gazed at me with adoration for a moment before I turned and followed my boss out into the hall where several security guards waited.

I was sure steam was coming out of Matthew's ears. He was so angry I could feel it radiating off him. He was the one who said to eat before work. Hypocrite.

Matthew didn't stop until he was on the elevator. So, I followed him on. The security guards didn't follow. As the door slid shut, I saw Thor give me a half grin. There was something weird about that guy.

"What was the first rule, Ren?" Matthew asked, voice carefully controlled.

"I don't know, you have so many of them," I replied, leaning back against the wall of the elevator. My heart was still beating, and I was flying high.

"Do not eat the guests," he said, his voice punctuating each word like a shot.

"Well, you are the one who told me to eat before my shift. Am I supposed to go gallivanting around the city trying to find dinner with no money and no car?"

My argument was pretty weak. My heart gave one last beat and stopped again. All my limbs were warm and tingly.

"How long have you been on this restrictive diet?"

I was high enough that my lips were loose. "Since I turned nineteen."

"Holy shit," he whispered.

I realized I had said the words out loud and wished I could grab them out of the air and swallow them back down.

"You have been starving yourself for 200 years?" He hit the stop button on the elevator.

"Not starving myself. I just eat when I need to. It's not a big deal. Shut up."

He stared at me like I had two heads. I tried to push past him and hit the button to make the elevator go, but he blocked it with his body.

"Stop!" I backed into the corner of the elevator and trained my eyes on the patterned carpet floor. Everything had gone to shit. I didn't want him to keep looking at me like that. Finally, I heard him turn and push the button on the elevator and we started moving again. When the door opened, we were on the top floor. Matthew disappeared out the door and I waited a moment longer. When I followed, he wasn't in the hall.

I went to my suite and collapsed inside the door. Bloody tears fell from my eyes and landed softly on the tile in the entryway. After a few moments, I slipped my shoes off and took a deep breath. Then I pushed myself up and walked into the bathroom. Washing my face, I felt more like myself again.

I got changed into my uniform and walked back out the door. Hopefully, I could just pretend nothing happened and Matthew would do me the courtesy of doing the same.

ELEVEN

Down on the casino floor, Carson found me. He led me to a table near the back, but not as far back as last time. I took over between deals as the woman who was dealing had three people sitting at her table.

Those people sat staring at me so I began. I dealt while the two men and a woman chatted about politics and the weather. One player was watching my hands like a hawk. His eyes darted every time I moved to pick a card or set one down. I used my left hand to move chips, and he noticed and got a twitch in his eye.

Thor came and stood beside me, so I stopped messing around and just dealt the cards. Thor moved on. I saw Carson a few times as he circulated or moved the staff around.

My table had traffic almost all shift and by the time I finished my shift my fingers were sore from sliding and flipping cards.

"Good work tonight, Ren," Carson said with a smile on his face as I stopped in at the employee lounge to punch out.

"Thanks, Carson."

"Listen, don't get too comfortable here. You are smart and need to do something more with your life than deal cards. Don't get set in your ways."

He gave me a salute and went back to the floor. I wondered how long he had been working at the casino. It was easy for a vampire to get set in their ways and never change. They become mean and bitter like my father. The reminder made me uncomfortable.

I went up to my suite to change. I needed to get out and relax.

I changed into some new clothes and hit the street as fast as my legs would carry me.

It was night time again, but the city was so well lit between the streetlights, the flashing lights on the casino and the headlights of the traffic, I couldn't find a shadow to hide in.

I walked down the strip soaking in the atmosphere and trying to figure out which bars looked most likely to welcome vampires. I wandered about until I came upon a chapel; it was kind of small, but I walked up the steps and pulled open the door.

Inside it looked like a miniature version of Father John's chapel. There were only a few rows of pews and a pulpit at the front, and a couple of people stood to one side.

I continued to the front pew and made the sign of the cross. I didn't see a confessional, so I just approached the priest. He looked like Elvis. It worked for him.

"Forgive me Father for I have sinned. It has been four days since my last confession." Was it just four days?

I wasn't sure what day it was. I held up a finger to tell him to wait, took out my phone and checked. "Yup, four days."

"Uhm, I was just about to marry these folks over here," the priest said, in a heavy southern drawl.

"I'll just be a minute," I said, looking back at the couple. When I smiled at them, they took a step back.

I turned my toothy grin on the priest.

He said a prayer that wasn't like Father John's, but it was pretty and lyrical. Like a song. "What's your name?"

"Ren," I replied.

"Ok, Ren looks like I have a few minutes."

"So, at least four times I have lied. Including once telling Jenkins that I thought the t-shirt he bought me was funny. Twice I gave people the finger. I purposely scared several people including the plumber," I laughed, remembering Henry's face. Hooking my thumb over my shoulder at the couple by the door, I said, "I think I scared them too. And once I drank from a man in the casino even though I'm not supposed to drink from people in the casino. My new boss is overwhelming. He has so many rules."

When the priest said nothing, I looked at him.

"There's no job too immense when you've got confidence," he whispered. I wasn't sure if he was talking to me or himself.

"So, what should I do? Father John always tells me what to do."

"Uhm, ok, so, don't do those things anymore and maybe say some Our Fathers?" he said unsurely.

"Are you asking me or telling me?"

"Which do you prefer?" he asked. He was a terrible priest.

"You are supposed to tell me. You know, counsel me on how to live better," I replied.

"Ok, I'm telling you then." He didn't sound like Elvis at all. I was positive Elvis would have been sure the first time.

"Ok, thank you Father," I said.

"You know I'm not a real Priest, right?"

"That's Ok. I don't believe in God," I said as I got up and walked back out of the little chapel. I'd have to remember how I got here so I could come back next week.

———

I found a small nightclub with crowds of people. The music had a good beat and lots of dark corners. Most importantly, the bar welcomed vampires. I knew this because it was called Vein. Nobody called their club something so obvious unless it was advertising to my fellow biters and those looking for a nice bite.

They set the club up with a bar running halfway around the space and the rest was all dance-floor. Bar stools lined the bar, but no other seating. I ordered a vampire fire, and they delivered promptly. Just my kind of place.

I downed my drink and went out to dance for a while.

Dancing was fun, but not as fun when I wasn't hunting, so, after a few songs, I left the club and promised myself to come back the next time I wanted to dine. The short walk to the Casino flew past in a daze of lights and sounds. Before I knew it, I was walking through the lobby. As I walked past the coffee shop though, I saw the kid with the laptop. He was madly typing away on his keyboard, completely ignoring everyone around him.

I walked in and snuck up behind him. HA, gotcha! He was typing away on an SQL injection. Trying to hack someone's bank account.

"I can do better," I said.

He jumped and tried to get out of his seat, but I put my hands on his shoulders and held him down. Then whispered in his ear.

"Let me help you and in return, you can help me. I can get you a shit ton of cash, I just need access to your laptop. Don't run, ok?"

His shoulders were bony, but he was stronger than I had expected. He nodded, and I released him.

"Are there cameras in here?" I asked him as I slid into the seat beside him.

He shook his head. Perfect.

"Let me see?"

He turned the laptop towards me and I thought he would make a break for it. The laptop must have more value to him than his life, because he stayed put, but sat on the edge of his seat.

I rolled through the SQL combinations until I mucked up the thing enough and got into the account. I turned the laptop back to the kid, stood up and walked out of the coffee shop. Hopefully, he would be back tomorrow and maybe less afraid of me. He was in fight-or-flight mode right now. I needed his heart rate much lower and his head much clearer if I was going to get some work out of him.

Up in my suite, I showered and changed into some comfy pants and the big Texas t-shirt Jenkins had bought me. Yeah, I hated it, but it reminded me of home. I curled up on the couch and flicked around channels on the TV until I found the soaps. Humans were endless hours of entertainment.

———

A pounding on my door woke me up. I untwisted myself from my blanket and staggered to the door with only one eye open, wiping the drool off the side of my face.

I flung the door open and before me was a perfectly coiffed Matthew. His hair was immaculate and his soft green dress shirt made his blue eyes pop. I straightened my shirt and tried to smooth it out a bit. Then realized my hair was a rat's nest.

Ugh.

"What?" I asked, annoyed now that I looked like trash and he was at my door.

"Your shift started 5 minutes ago."

I scrunched up my nose. "I'm sick."

"You are a vampire, you don't get sick, Ren. Get moving."

I tried to shut the door, but he pushed his way in. I grumbled things that didn't make sense and then spent five minutes in a hot shower wishing I was dead...deader.

When I walked back out in my uniform, tying my hair up into a bun, Matthew was sitting on my couch watching the news.

They were talking about Ed and how the Blood Guard couldn't pin anything on him because their witnesses always turned up dead.

"You going to sit here all day?" I asked.

He clicked off the TV.

"You didn't have to wait for me," I said. "I know my way to the casino floor."

"I thought you might forget the way since your memory seems to be lax," he said with a smile. Was he joking around with me? That was unsettling. "You know the hotel has a wake-up service."

That sounded handy. I had always set my own schedule when I was self-employed...I laughed out loud at that thought. Self-employed.

"What's so funny?" Matthew asked.

"Nothing," I said.

———

Over the next few days, I got into a regular routine. I went to work, then back to my suite and slept.

Then, one morning, I saw him. The kid with the laptop. The table I was running was close to the door, and I watched as the kid walked in and set up in the coffee shop across the hall. I messed up a few deals and Thor came and stood beside me.

"I need to get off work early," I said to him after I finished dealing a hand.

He turned and left without a word. About five minutes later, Carson walked over with another dealer who promptly took over for me. That was easy.

I turned to leave, but Thor grabbed my arm. I looked at his hand and then up to his face and raised a brow.

"Boss wants to know why."

"Female problems," I said with a straight face.

Thor stared at me for a moment, but his eyes lost focus like he was listening to someone on his earpiece. Probably Matthew.

His eyes refocused on my face and his hand let go of me. He turned and walked away. That was easy too. I looked up at the camera above me and gave him a thumbs up, then walked out of the casino and into the coffee shop.

The kid was waiting for me. His eyes got big, but he didn't try to run this time. He moved back in his seat as I approached.

"Hi there. Can I borrow your laptop for a second?"

He didn't say anything, just spun the laptop towards me. There was a word document open, and it said. "I don't speak. My name is Ben. Can you show me how you did that?"

"You don't speak?" I asked.

He shook his head no. That was weird but oddly convenient. I didn't have to listen to him talk.

"Perfect," I said.

He reached over and hit a button and the screen came up to another bank webpage.

"I need to do something and then I'll show you how to do that."

I downloaded my hacking software bundle from the cloud and installed it on the kid's computer. It would take a while and I didn't want to sit in here all night. I'd have to run it next time.

Once that was downloading, I pulled the account back up that the kid was hacking and went through step by step how to blast the password.

When I got him in the account, there was only three thousand dollars, but the kid happily transferred in out.

"You didn't just put that in your personal account, did you?"

Ben opened the notepad up and typed "No, I'm not an idiot."

"Ok, sorry," I said. "I'll meet you back here tomorrow. Don't fuck with that program I'm installing. You mess it up, I will bite you." I said, snapping my teeth at the kid, whose eyes got as big as saucers. I turned and went up to my suite.

Vampires didn't get female problems, but I was cold and tired, which was a problem, and I am female. It was Saturday morning, and I had two days off in a row.

I spent the morning in the sauna, soaking up all the heat and listening to the humans' chatter. It was usually as good as watching soaps. All the drama of their lives spilled into the room like the steam out of the hot rocks in the corner. But eventually, I dragged myself away from the heat to get ready for the evening. I needed something new to wear, I was tired of wearing the same couple of outfits and wanted to fit into the crowd in the nightclub.

I walked into the boutique. Deb was standing at the counter ringing up a sale for a middle-aged woman, so I looked through the racks of clothes. I needed something a bit slutty for the club. Not too over the top, but I wanted to have a fun night. I found a soft pink long sleeve dress that was form fitting, with an off-theshoulder neck line. The hem would be mid-thigh, but the material was tight and stretchy, so I could pull it up to make it shorter.

I grabbed one in my size and a pair of strappy shoes with a heel and waved at Deb as I sailed past to try it on. Squeezing myself into it, I slipped on the shoes and stepped out to check myself in the full-length mirror.

I heard a breath catch behind me and turned to find Matthew staring like he had never seen a girl before.

"I had heard stories that you were the most magnificent creature to walk the night, but I had thought them exaggerated," he whispered. I spun back around to try to hide the blood rising in my cheeks, but I faced the mirror and his eyes locked on mine again. I swallowed and shook my head.

"Did you need something?" I asked breaking eye contact and checking myself in the mirror. The most magnificent creature to walk the night?

He didn't speak for a moment but finally asked: "Why did you leave work early?"

"I wanted to take care of a few things." I looked at him again in the mirror while adjusting the hem of the dress to get it the right height.

He nodded. "Don't make it a habit." He turned on his heel and walked out of the change room.

Deb walked in a moment later.

"Did you find what you were looking for?" She asked, looking me up and down.

"I'd say so. Put it on Matthew's tab," I said as I pulled off the tag and handed it to her. I walked back out of the store, then out of the casino and down the street. My shoes would be ruined after tonight, anyway.

A night in the club was not kind to pretty shoes.

I walked up to the club, and the bouncer looked me up and down. I smiled at him and he opened the door and held it for me with a fanged smile in return. The club was already full with a line up outside.

This would be perfect.

TWELVE

I walked through the bar and eyes flashed in the strobe lights. I was like a safe harbour in a storm, calling the humans towards me. But I was no safe harbour. My prey drive was high tonight. I didn't want any of the men whose eyes tracked me across the room; I wanted to hunt. I sat down at the bar and the bartender set a drink in front of me. I hadn't ordered one, and when I looked up the bartender pointed down the bar and I saw Matthew, of all people, sitting at the bar. I toasted him and then turned my eyes back to the crowd of people dancing.

There were men of all descriptions here. The shirtless muscle-bound men and the dark-haired artistic types. There were cute boys with floppy hair and some very serious young men and women who were probably disciples. Thankfully, they didn't recognize me as a vampire. The perks of a new city.

I waited and watched, but my eyes kept tracking back to Matthew. He was hunting too. There was no mistaking the fire in his eyes as he watched the girls dancing.

He had dressed down tonight. His t-shirt was form fitting but his slacks still said, wealthy businessman. I let my eyes linger on his profile. His strong jaw was square and masculine but his nose had a nearly feminine quality that was at odds to his jaw and a sloped forehead. It intrigued me. The way it softened his face, making him a bit pretty.

His eyes flashed to mine, and I looked away, scanning the room like I wasn't just drooling over my boss, who is also an old vampire. I needed to give my head a shake. I finished my second drink and left my bar stool behind to dance with the young beautiful people with heartbeats. Their warmth was intoxicating as I danced between them. The room filled with the scents of aftershave and perfume and alcohol. As I moved closer to the DJ, the music was louder. I looked up at the DJ and his head was nodding to the music and keeping everyone moving with quick beats and smooth changes. The lights cycled through from colourful lasers to white strobes that made everyone move in stop-motion, animating the dancers around me like old movies. It was surreal and magical and I was maybe a bit drunk, I realized. I laughed at my own romanticizing of the nightclub as a pair of arms wrapped around me from behind. I didn't care who it was, they could dance. I danced for hours and realized I still hadn't found my prey.

I peeked behind me to find I had been dancing with a delicious looking human. He fell comfortably into the cute boy category. His flopsy hair was stuck to his forehead with sweat and his bare, chiseled chest glistened and rippled with muscle. Instead of wandering off to find my dinner, I chose him. I smiled at him and he tipped his head. I slid my arms around his sweat-slicked back and ran the tip of my nose from his collarbone to his ear. I wanted to take him out of here, but I wasn't sure if there was a back door. I took his hand and walked him out the front door instead.

I winked at the bouncer as I led my dinner outside. The bouncer chuckled. The night felt cold compared to the heat inside and my yummy snack shivered as I pushed him up against the side of the building once we rounded the corner in the alley.

"I'm Tim," he said.

Pressing my nose into his collarbone, I replied, "I don't care." My teeth slid through skin and muscle and vein. His whole body tensed and then loosened like a rag doll as his head tipped back against the brick and lolled to the side. His blood was like heavy silk, pouring down my throat and soothing all my cares away. I pressed into him to keep him upright against the wall. He would probably have scrapes on his back; I didn't care about that either. I felt my heart beat in my chest and I reluctantly licked his neck wound closed.

My heart continued to beat as I steadied Tim and then pulled him away from the wall and towards a waiting taxi. I stuffed him in the back seat and then reached back in and pulled out his wallet. He had a condom and a stick of gum. Well, that's not going to cut it.

"I've got it." Matthew handed the cabbie some money and then stepped back from the car. I stuffed Tim's wallet back in his pocket and shut the door.

"Thanks," I said.

"Your heart is still beating," he said.

I took Matthew's hand and pulled him back inside the club. In hindsight it was stupid, but at that moment, I would have killed anyone who got between me and him. I wrapped my arms around his shoulders and danced with him to the beat of my heart. It pounded in my ears like the bass to the music. It moved my body against Matthew's, demanding I don't let him go, lest I shatter into a million pieces. I felt alive.

But I wasn't alive. I was still dead. Eventually, my heart stopped beating and my brain took over the thinking. I let Matthew go. The crowd swallowed me up until I lost sight of him completely and I danced with the humans who didn't notice the bloody tear that fell from my cheek. I wiped the evidence away, and it was like it had never been there in the first place.

It wasn't much later when I left the club. The walk to the casino was a blur of lights and people. I found myself on the couch in my suite, in my baggy Texas tshirt, watching reruns of The Young and the Restless.

THIRTEEN

Sunday I spent waiting for my little hacker. I sat at the bar in the casino, positioned so I could see the doorway to the coffee shop. Carson made his rounds, and I watched as armed men came and picked up the deposit. They were led by Thor, who scanned the room constantly, his hand on the gun he kept in a holster beneath his jacket. I doubted he needed a weapon, considering how big he was. Add in his vampire strength and he could probably do a lot of damage to a would-be robber.

Finally, I saw Ben walk into the coffee shop and set up his laptop. I casually got up and wove my way past the card tables and slot machines.

"Oof," I bumped right into a solid chest. I looked up into Matthew's startling green eyes.

"Sorry, I wasn't looking where I was going," he said, but he also didn't move out of my way. I raised an eyebrow at him and he stepped to the side.

"See you later," I said as I walked past him and out of the casino. I looked over my shoulder and he was still watching me, so I walked around the corner towards the elevators.

When I was out of sight I stopped and waited. After a moment I peeked back into the casino. Carson and Matthew were standing where I had left him, discussing something. He needed to move along. I didn't want either of them to notice me walk into the coffee shop and come snooping around. I waited a few more minutes, admiring the painting that decorated the lobby wall, then peeked in. They had disappeared, so I turned to go to the coffee shop.

"What are you doing?" Matthew asked, startling me. God, he was a freaking ninja.

"Nothing, what are you doing? Following me?"

"No, I was just going up to my suite." He pointed towards the elevators.

"Ok, see ya later," I said walking out towards the front doors.

I peeked back as I walked through the revolving door and watched him get on the elevator. The door closed behind him, so I just kept revolving until I was back inside the casino, then walked briskly to the coffee shop before I was spotted by any other nosey person.

Inside I found Ben in a corner, hunched over his laptop. I slid in beside him and he jumped. His heart rate shot up before he realized it was me and he blew out a puff of air. He was like a deer: slim, leggy and nervous as all heck.

"Hi, got my download?"

He spun the laptop towards me and hit a key, bringing up my software package. Glorious, beautiful revenge in the form of code.

I sighed and grabbed a newspaper someone had helpfully left on one of the other tables in the coffee shop.

I flipped through until I found what I was looking for. A man named Andrew Linton was accused of embezzling funds from the Sick Kids Hospital Foundation. I wondered how he would like his funds siphoned off. I began the process of tracking him down. He was on social media, had dating profiles, as well as a public profile and contact information on the hospital Foundation's page.

Ben watched as I typed. His eyes danced like he was trying to memorize every keystroke. He was sharp, and I was willing to bet he had the general idea of everything I was doing and could probably do some mean social hacking by the time I was finished demonstrating.

"You don't do this on your own," I said to him.

He nodded.

I was pretty sure he was going to try it. I just hoped he didn't ruin my program. I had paid a lot for it on the dark web.

Soon I had everything sent out, and then it was just a waiting game, so I logged out and turned the laptop back to Ben.

"I'll see you tomorrow," I said. I stood and turned, but Ben slapped the table and I turned back to him. He held up a finger to me in the universal signal to wait.

He typed quickly and spun his laptop for me to read.

It read, "I need money."

"What do you need money for?" I asked.

He spun the laptop back again, and typed something else. I walked back to look over his shoulder. "Rent."

"You just stole from someone the other day." He was lying, but his big light blue eyes blinked at me with innocence. Yeah, he was good at that look. I bet it worked for him often and if not yet, it would soon. When he started to fill out, he was going to be a heartbreaker.

"Fine, I'll transfer you some tomorrow when we get that guy." I walked out and returned to my suite, hoping to nap until I had to get back to work on Monday, but as I lay on the couch, the bathroom tap dripping broke my peaceful quiet. Like Chinese water torture. I couldn't stand it.

Finally, I called down to the front desk, and they assured me someone would be up right away to fix it.

I waited by the door, with the lights off in the suite and curtains shut. The elevator doors opened with a soft ding, then the jingle of tools that counted out a rhythm in time with heavy foot-steps and laboured breathing moved towards my door.

The sounds stopped and a man's voice whispered 1204, which was my suite number. Knuckles rapped on the door twice.

I stood out of sight and slowly opened the door like a classic scary movie. The door obliged my theatrics by making a drawn-out, squeaky sound.

Once the door was fully open, I could see the large man standing in the hall through the crack between the hinges. He hadn't moved and had a look on his face like he was having a heart attack. I waited to see what he would do.

After another moment he said "H..hello?"

I had to cover my mouth to keep the laughter at bay.

He took a step forward. Then another. "Hello?" he called again.

"Shit," he whispered. "What are you doing, Henry? It's just like every other room."

He took two more steps in and reached for the light. I threw the door shut, slamming it hard. The loud noise made Henry drop his tools and spin around much faster than I imagined his large frame capable of.

I flicked on the lights and stood in a regal pose, like the vampires in old black and white movies. Classic. Henry's heart was apparently better than I thought.

He laughed uncomfortably at himself and picked up his tools, keeping his eyes on me like I might still jump on him or produce some weapon.

"You scared me there," he chuckled.

"Apologies." I smiled, making sure my teeth were fully visible.

"Uhm, you have a leaky tap?" He shifted from foot to foot, still completely uncomfortable.

"Yes, in the bathroom," I said pointing towards the bedroom.

"Ok, I'll get that fixed right up for you." He shuffled off quickly, and I covered my mouth so my laughter wouldn't spill out. Then went to the couch and sat down.

Henry was not a quiet man. There was a surprising amount of banging and swearing for what I assumed was just a quick fix. But the bathroom sink seemed to be putting up quite a fight. I was just amusing myself with counting the number of times he dropped the fbomb when there was another knock at my door.

I got up and peeked out the peephole to find Matthew standing there. I opened the door.

"Hey, how's it going?" I asked to the soundtrack of Henry swearing and banging.

Matthew gave me a questioning look. "What is going on in there?"

"Just my lover. He's really into some kinky stuff."

"You better not have him here against his will," Matthew said just as Henry must have got the tap off because he let out a resounding "Yes!"

I bit my lip to keep a straight face.

Matthew's face contorted into a mask of disgust. "Is there someone else in there with him?"

I channeled my inner Zen before I opened my mouth again. "No."

"There you go, how do you like that?" Henry asked, I assumed, the sink. "That's better, isn't it?" The sound of tools being put away and the water running on and off came from his direction before Henry came walking back out of my bedroom.

"That should keep you," he said. "Oh, Hello Mr. Merewin." Henry walked past us both and out to the elevators.

I burst out laughing. I couldn't hold it back anymore. God, Matthew's face had been priceless.

Matthew pushed me back into the suite and shut the door.

"Why are you like this?" he asked. I was laughing too hard to answer. Not that I had an answer for him. It was funny. That was enough.

He shook his head. "Anyway, I have to go check on one of my businesses out of town and wondered if you would join me."

"You afraid I'll get into trouble if you leave me here by myself?" I asked, wiping the tears of laughter from my eyes.

"My presence doesn't seem to have any effect on your behavior. I would like to have some company."

I sobered at that. "Why would you want my company?" I asked.

"Why wouldn't I want your company?"

"You can't lie to a liar," I replied.

"Fine, I'm having some issues with the local vampires. I would like you to come as a show of force. If they think I'm paired, they will stop pushing my claim."

I snorted. Typical. "Fine, whatever," I said. At least he wasn't trying to convince me it was because of my winning personality.

———

Matthew drove a red Corolla. I mean, it was a new one, still had the new car smell, but it was a Corolla.

"Why don't you have a nicer car?" I asked. I didn't know how to judge Matthew based on this choice of a reliable, smooth-driving mid-size car.

"This is a perfectly fine car. It's well rated."

My eyes rolled of their own volition. I missed Priscilla and wondered if Brian had finished fixing the front end. Probably. Maybe I could find his account information and send him some money.

The freeway's traffic was fairly light today, but the Corolla cruised along at the speed limit.

"How far is this place?" I asked after an extended silence that Matthew didn't seem interested in filling.

"Not much farther," he said cryptically.

I sighed and went back to looking out the window.

"How did you get your own city without being paired?" I asked.

He smiled. "I'm pretty old."

I narrowed my eyes at him. "How old?"

"Pushing a millennium."

"Yeah, you're pretty old." My father was at least 3 times that. The only vampire older than my father lived and ruled in Europe.

"Thanks," he said as he flicked on his turn indicator and moved to the off ramp. I was distracted by the small town we drove into. There was a street of old houses, a corner store and a church. I could see clear across the town, even in the low evening light.

Matthew parked the car and got out. I followed him to the front door of an older house. A few moments after he knocked, the door opened and a little old woman stood hunched in the doorway.

"Ah, Matthew, dear. Come in, come in."

"Hello, Margret. Thank you." We walked into a parlour with antique furniture I was willing to bet was original to the house. "Allow me to introduce you to Ren."

"Oh, my, aren't you beautiful," the woman said as she adjusted her glasses on her nose with shaking hands and peered at me. She looked back at Matthew and smiled.

"How have you been?" Matthew asked.

"Oh, I'm fine," she waved him off and looked at me. "Our Matthew is always so considerate, isn't he? I suppose I don't have to tell you that." She giggled like a school girl.

"No, I guess not," I said, turning my eyes to Matthew and raising an eyebrow. He sat stone-faced like there was nothing weird about this situation.

"You know, since my Arnie died, I have been rambling around in this old house all alone. I love it when Matthew comes to visit." She smiled at me and in the silence, her heart skipped a beat and another before it settled into a rhythm again. The old woman was dying. She had to be in her nineties. I had no idea who this human woman was to Matthew, but she wasn't going to be here long.

I sat back in my chair and the old woman droned on about her husband. He was a carpenter and worked every day from the time they were married at sixteen until the day he died.

I would never die. Probably.

After an hour or so of stories from the old woman's life, Matthew told her we had to get back to the city but thanked her for letting us visit. The woman gushed some more about Matthew and then pinched my cheek.

"I hope you will be as happy with Matthew as I was with Arnie," she whispered conspiratorially. When she looked back at Matthew, he winked at her.

We walked out to the car, and a tear fell from my eye. I wiped it away quickly, got in the car and slammed the door. Rage blew through me like fire in a hayloft. Hot and fast and fierce. It replaced the sadness, and I didn't try to temper it. Being angry was easy.

Matthew didn't say anything, he just got in and steered the car out of town towards the freeway.

"Why did you bring me here?" I asked through gritted teeth. "What kind of game are you playing?" I was shouting now. My voice hoarse from my efforts to control my anger.

"Why are you angry?" he asked in an even tone.

"Why am I angry? Are you kidding? You lied to me!"

"No, Ren, I told you the truth, but you didn't believe me. So, I told you a version of the truth that you expected."

I smashed my hand on the dashboard, then crossed my arms and turned to look out the window.

"It's ok Ren."

I didn't reply. He was making everything worse.

"It's ok."

"Shut up," I growled.

"It's ok to be sad."

"You shut your mouth, Matthew! You have no idea what you are talking about."

I was cold all of a sudden. I pulled my feet up onto the seat and wrapped my arms around my knees. Then buried my face in them and locked out the world.

When the car rolled to a stop, I looked up and found I was in the parking garage beside the casino. I opened the door and marched back to my suite. Left Matthew in my dust and wrote the whole day off as a waste.

I had a few hours before my shift so got into my swimsuit and marched down to the sauna. There were a couple people mulling about inside but I hissed at them and they promptly left.

The air was damp already but hot, so I sat in the corner and leaned back, resting my head on the woodpaneled wall.

A sneaky tear slipped out and made a trail down my face. I wiped it with my hand and then studied the bloody smear on my palm. I watched as it slowly dried.

Leaving just a stain of pink where it had been.

The lifeblood.

The only thing that held my existence.

My corpse.

FOURTEEN

That night I finished my shift, changed into street clothes and walked out the front door of the casino.

I marched down the crowded strip. When they said the city never sleeps, they weren't exaggerating. We were made for each other, Las Vegas and I.

I turned into the little white church and pushed through the doors. Music played, it sounded nice, but not like at the church services I had been to.

I walked toward the pulpit where a couple stood. The priest stopped talking, the man and woman turned to look at me.

"I need to talk to you, Father Elvis."

"Can you wait 'til I'm done here, little lady? I'll only be a minute." His accent was more pronounced this time.

"Sure, I'll just sit here," I said, stepping into one of the tiny pews and sitting down. The floor at my feet was new, not worn like in Father John's church. In fact, the whole floor was shiny and new looking. The walls were painted white, and the windows had stained glass guitars in them instead of the Virgin Mary and Christ on the cross.

I waited while Father Elvis blessed the union of the happy couple. Then he sang a song and the couple left.

I walked up to the pulpit and knelt down.

"Bless me, Father, for I have sinned. It has been a week since my last confession. I lied to my boss, yelled at him, and scared the plumber. I also hissed at some people in the sauna, but one of them had a terrible laugh, so I don't think that was a sin. Jesus would have told her to go away, too."

"A little less fight and a little more spark. Close your mouth and open your heart," he said in a bit of a melody. It didn't make much sense, but sometimes Father John spoke in riddles too.

"Thank you, Father Elvis. I'm also having trouble with my boss. He keeps asking questions and provoking me. It's like he wants me to go crazy."

"When things go wrong, don't go with 'em."

"Yeah, all right. Uhm do you want me to say some Our Fathers and stuff?" I asked. I was more confused than when I had walked in.

"Sure, whatever you like," he said.

"Thank you."

I didn't feel lighter. If anything, I was heavier, the weight of eternity pressing down on me. I walked out to wander the city like I used to do before nightclubs made hunting so easy.

———

By the 1920s prohibition was in full swing, but that didn't stop the people from drinking nor did it stop me from dining on the drunks. Back then I was a bit dramatic.

I stalked my prey down the streets of Chicago. My feet were light on the sidewalk. The man wore a heavy wool coat. It was almost Christmas, and I was cold. He weaved through the crowds of shoppers, dashing in and out of the shops. Their parcels, wrapped in glittery paper and trailing ribbons, overflowed their bags. The country was bountiful and people were living well for that blink of time between the end of World War I and the Great Depression. A great time to be American. The man I stalked wore a finely-made, shiny top hat, displaying his wealth.

I watched him earlier in the speakeasy, laughing and joking with his friends as they drank. He spoke confidently and laughed in a self-assured way. I craved him. My teeth longed for his neck, but I needed to get him alone -- to single him out and keep him for myself. I hunted him like a lioness on the plains of Africa, moving in as close as I dared.

As he turned a corner, I hurried to catch up, dashing around the corner, and bumped right into him.

"Well, hello there," he said, his voice like silk. It floated on the night air.

"Oh, I'm so sorry," I dropped my chin so he wouldn't see my teeth. Before vampires came out to the humans, we still hid our teeth.

"It's a pleasure bumping into you, I assure you, but why are you following me?" he asked.

He put his finger under my chin, lifting my face into the streetlight for his inspection.

"You are exquisite. Would you like to come home with me?" he asked. He was drunk, so I agreed. Drunk men were easy targets, and they always passed out after I had finished.

He slid my arm under his and led me down the cold streets to his house. It was a narrow two-story house tucked up between two others. The row of identical brick-faced houses lined the street. He led me inside and stoked the fire, making the room deliciously warm. I lounged on the chaise until he returned.

"Would you like a drink?" he asked.

I nodded, and he smiled. There was a small counter in the far end of the room with decanters and glasses. His casual disregard of the law just made me long for him all the more. He returned with two glasses and we toasted.

"So, tell me about yourself," he said, sitting down beside me and resting his arm around the back of the couch. He was easy to talk to. We spoke of many things that night; from favourite drink to politics. Of course, I lied and told him gin was my favourite drink. I enjoyed speaking to him and sitting in front of the fire.

"Do you want to bite me?" he asked, shocking me out of the quiet that had fallen on us.

"What do you mean?" I asked.

"You are a vampire, right? That's why you followed me. I was bitten a few years ago, though I don't remember much of it. If you want to bite me, you can." He moved closer, his cocky smile rather endearing. I took him up on his offer and he was as delicious as I had imagined. I stayed with him that night and the next. Another month passed and soon it was spring. I had bitten Edward several times, holed up in his row house. We spent most nights wrapped in blankets together in front of the fire.

"I have to leave soon," I told him one sunny day. The tulips had flowered, and my family was moving south. Staying indoors all winter had almost driven me mad.

"You can't. Please, Nia. You can stay here for the summer. Don't leave!" He wrapped his arms around me and sobbed like a child.

I had broken him.

The following day I left while he was out at the market. He was handsome and wonderful but humans couldn't handle being bitten more than once. I had sinned and the handsome man I once pined for had become a shadow of himself.

Later, I read in a news article that he had jumped from the top of the Home Insurance Building to his death.

I walked down the Strip to the nightclub Vein. The music was pounding, and the line was long. I walked up to the bouncer and he moved the rope that blocked the humans from entering and then held the door for me. I winked at him and walked through.

Ordering two drinks at the bar, I downed the first one fast, letting the pure alcohol burn through my throat and down to my stomach. I drank the second one even faster, giving myself a light buzz. Then I lost myself on the dance floor. Bodies and limbs moved and shook like an earthquake. The lights flashed in different colours making my eyes struggle to see, but I didn't need to see. The music was so loud, it felt like my heart was beating in my chest and I felt alive. I let my mind shut off. I didn't care about vampires or humans or old ladies who had done more living in one life than I would ever accomplish in a millennia. Hands caressed my body and the scent of pine and vodka reached my nose. I fell into the moment, turning and twisting with the collective dance.

Eyes tracked me; gaging, hunting eyes. And when I looked in the direction of the intent stare, I found Matthew. I left my eyes locked on his and moved against the body behind me. Matthew's eyes traced my features and then followed my body down to my feet. Goosebumps rose on my flesh. He was hunting and didn't try to hide it.

His eyes would dart from me to a blonde. Her hair traced the top of her ass and her skirt barely covered it. I moved across the dance floor to be near her. When I danced beside her, she smiled at me. Her features were delicate, like a flower in perfect bloom. Her skin was so pale, we could be twins and when I put my arm around her thin waist, she moved her body with mine in perfect harmony.

I watched over her shoulder, Matthew's eyes burned with fire and desire. I had his prize in my grasp. He had been stalking her, but she was in my arms. I held his eyes as I flashed my fangs at her and she tipped her head.

Time stopped.

I held Matthew's eyes as I licked her lavender scented neck.

Goosebumps rose on her hot flesh.

Matthew licked his lips.

I slid my fangs through her milky skin and into the vein pumping her life through her body. The rush of salty tang slid down my throat and I closed my eyes as it warmed my mouth. When my eyes opened again, Matthew stood before me, his prize sandwiched between us. His Adam's apple bobbed in jealousy. Mine bobbed a swallow of the nectar from his victim. I drank my fill, his eyes intent on mine like he could know how she tasted by watching me. I closed the wound and let her go.

Matthew pulled me to his arms and roughly sealed his mouth on mine. Like a man dying of thirst, his tongue scrapped the inside of my mouth but the meal was beyond his reach. It filled my veins now. It pumped to the wakened will of my heart.

He released me and spun, leaving the dance floor as the music came back to my ears and the rest of the room came back to my awareness.

I danced, embracing the beat of the music as it tried to compete with the pounding in my chest. But it was just a momentary lapse. An escape from the eternal stillness.

When my heart finally stopped beating, I walked back to the casino alone.

FIFTEEN

I had intended to go to my suite and watch soaps, but the casino lights caught my eye and I followed my feet to a poker table. One particularly slow night, I had watched the table and figured out the rules of the game.

I slid a crisp twenty-dollar bill out of my purse and handed it to the woman working the table. She pushed back a stack of chips.

"Ante," she said.

The others at the table tossed a chip in the middle so I followed suit.

She then dealt out the cards and each of us peeked at our own while she set out three more cards in the center of the table, face down.

A few of the other players tossed in coins so I did as well.

As the dealer revealed the cards, I found I didn't have any type of hand and planned to fold, but instead I couldn't stop myself from calling. As the last card was turned over, I pushed all my chips into the center. My hands, working against my better sense.

The only man still playing tossed his cards in the middle and the dealer pushed all the coins towards me.

Interesting.

I continued to play several more hands, some I folded and others I called, but I invariably made more and more money. That is until Thor appeared at my elbow. I looked up into his dark eyes.

"The boss would like to see you."

"No doubt," I muttered. I left my chips on the table since I didn't need the money. I had been paid for my work and it was more than I needed for alcohol.

Thor led me through the back hallways to Matthew's door.

As he raised his hand to knock, I pushed past him and opened the door. Matthew was expecting me, after all.

I walked in and slumped down in the chair across from Matthew, then kicked my booted feet up onto a stack of folders sitting on the corner of his desk. He ignored me, staring down at papers, his pen tapping on the desk surface. I waited, examining my fingernails.

After several moments he stopped his incessant pen tapping and lifted his head. "Why are you playing poker in my casino?"

"I couldn't find any more tall blondes to drink," I replied, still examining my fingernails.

His pen snapped in two. I wasn't sure if he was angry or excited at the reminder of my thievery. Either emotion was fine with me.

"You shouldn't have done that," he whispered.

"Done what?" I looked up at his face and licked my lips slowly. His eyes tracked the movement and his eyelids lowered a fraction of an inch. I smiled, and he dropped his eyes back down to the papers on his desk.

He cleared his throat and said "You can't gamble in my casino. You work here. It's part of the rules if you remember."

I didn't listen to his rules, so I didn't know that, but there were hundreds of casinos in Las Vegas so it wasn't a big deal.

"Ok," I replied.

"Ok?"

"That means I accept your words and will abide by your rule," I rolled my eyes.

"Ok," he replied.

I stood to leave.

"Wait."

"What?" I said when he didn't speak.

"I'll see you tomorrow," he said, picking up and straightening the papers on his desk like that was what he had meant to say all along.

"Sure." I walked out the door and through the tunnels to the lobby, then took the elevator up to my suite. I changed and collapsed on the king size bed, pulling the heavy blankets over top of me. I wasn't cold, but the comfort of the cocoon held me together as I drifted off to sleep.

When I woke, rain was hitting the window. A flash of lightning that illuminated the room followed a rumble of thunder. I imagined the power it would take to shake the sky like that. A million running horses, or stomping sumo wrestlers.

I threw back the covers and got ready for my shift in the casino. My hair tied up in a bun and clad in my uniform, I walked down to the lobby.

Ben was standing there. He looked up when I got off the elevator and then held my eye and walked into the coffee shop. I only had five minutes, but I followed his obvious summons.

"What are you doing?" I asked as he sat down in a booth in the back corner.

He opened his laptop and his fingers flew over the keyboard, then turned the screen in my direction.

It read "I'm in trouble."

"What did you do?" I asked, clicking through to my program to make sure he hadn't messed it up. It seemed to be fine. When I looked back up at him, he had tears rimming his eyes and his lip quivered.

I turned the laptop back to him. He just sat there.

"Type," I commanded.

He jumped at my harsh tone and the tapping of keys filled the silence. He typed for a long time before he turned the laptop back.

The new words read, "I owe a lot of money to a man who will kill me if I don't pay him back. I borrowed money for my mother's hospital bills but she died and now I have nothing and the man keeps charging more and more interest."

"How much is a lot?" I asked him.

He typed. "500,000"

His tall lanky frame had crumpled into a ball like he wanted to disappear. This loan shark shouldn't have done business with a kid, even one with a sad story.

"All right, I have to go to work, but after my shift, I'll meet you here." Then I turned and went to work.

Carson led me to a table near the back. "Why am I all the way back here today?" I asked

"Boss' orders," Carson mumbled.

I laughed. Punishment for stealing his prize? I looked up at the camera in the ceiling and licked my lips, betting the man himself was watching. Then settled in for a night of doing nothing.

Near the end of my shift, a vampire walked in who didn't particularly look like he was there for a night of fun and relaxation. My neck prickled when his eyes locked on mine and he turned and walked to my table like he had been searching for me.

The man put a chip down and I dealt for him. When he lost, I saw him slide a note between the cards as he pushed them forward, then he stood up and left the casino. I raked them in and slipped the note into my pocket.

Thor showed up at my shoulder. I smiled at him but his stern face didn't change. He just watched me. My table was quiet for the rest of my shift and when it was over I walked out of the casino and up to my suite.

I locked the door behind me and took out the note.

It read: We have the kid. Bring 1 million dollars. Be in front of 44 Low Street in 24 hours. If you're late, the kid dies.

I wondered if they had his laptop. His IP was logged in my cloud server. A safeguard in case he took off with my software. I just needed a computer to track him down.

Operation Recover Ben's Laptop was a go.

I walked down to the lobby and out onto the casino floor. Then weaved through the tinkling slot machines and card tables until I found Thor.

"Can you ask Matthew to meet me in the coffee shop?" I asked him.

Thor put a finger to his earpiece and spoke in a hushed tone. His eyes got a faraway look for a second and then refocused on me. He nodded and then turned back to his surveying of the casino floor.

Step one complete.

I hustled into the boutique and stood behind a mannequin with a clear view of the hall. There, I waited for Matthew. I wouldn't have much time once he walked by.

"Can I help you?" Deb asked timidly.

"Shh," I replied, and she backed up a few steps. She would blow my cover. I hissed at her and she ran away. I stifled my laugh and reminded myself this was serious.

When Matthew walked by, heading for the coffee shop, I zipped out behind him and across the lobby to the door that led to the back hallways.

I had memorized the route to his office and ran the whole way, my feet slapping hard on the cement floor to gain time. I slipped through his office door and immediately walked to his desk. His computer was on and the video feed was of the casino floor.

Matthew was talking to Thor. Hopefully, that kept him busy. I minimized the program and logged into my cloud, grabbed the IP for Ben's laptop and logged into the dark web.

I posted a request to track and got a reply a few seconds later from someone who went by the name Stonewall. The bid was higher than the money in my bank account. I counter bid the exact dollar amount I had earned since I started here. He accepted, so I transferred the money and gave him the IP.

I tapped my fingers waiting for the results. Popping back up the window with the video feed, I saw Matthew had left. I hit the arrow keys to move from camera to camera but didn't see him anywhere. Finally, the computer pinged, and I switched back to the dark web.

Bingo.

I wrote down the address on a piece of paper, stood up and tucked it in my pocket, then logged off the dark web. Just as the office door opened and Matthew walked in, the computer screen went black. He stopped in his tracks and looked at me. I froze like a deer in headlights for a half a second and then did the only thing I could think. I undid the top button on my shirt. His eyes flashed down to my hands. I pulled my hair around to one shoulder, bearing my neck. He took a step closer, shutting the door behind him.

I turned on my super seductress and swaggered across the room to him.

"What are you doing?" he asked. His throat bobbed harshly.

I was already walking down the road, I wouldn't back out now. I stepped right up to him, so the coolness of his body mingled with mine. My neck was right in front of him, but he kept his eyes trained on mine.

He wrapped his hands around my upper arms and pulled me so our bodies touched but then he shuttered and pushed back a step, holding me at arm's reach.

I searched his face. Maybe I had gotten his signals wrong. I offer myself on a platter and he turns me down. Either way worked in this situation. I faked anger at his refusal. Let it show in my eyes before I shoved him out of the way and went racing out of his office.

The finest bit of acting I had ever accomplished, truth be told.

I laughed at how serious he had looked. I rounded the final corner and dashed through the casino then continued out onto the street. I walked to the city bus terminal and checked the map of the city. It didn't give street numbers, but I found the street and would have to take city transport to get there. My bank account was empty, not that it had held much money in the first place. When I got that laptop, I would have to stream cash into my account and get my own freaking laptop.
This was a ridiculous inconvenience.

I stood at the bus stop, next to a man with a bushy grey beard that smelled of rot and paint.

"You got any change?" he asked me. I still had a dollar and some coins in my pocket, the coins would get me on the bus, and the man smelled just terrible, so I held up the dollar bill.

He reached for it with grubby hands and I snatched it away.

"I'll give this to you if you go somewhere else until my bus arrives," I said.

He held out his hand for my bill, I put it within his reach and he grabbed it then went scurrying off like a rat in a tunnel, taking the smell with him.

Dollar well spent.

When the bus stopped in front of me, I stepped on and dropped the last of my money into the slot beside the driver. The coins jingled like a slot machine.

My pockets empty, I sat down behind the driver.

The city slid past in a haze of colour and sounds. Impatient drivers honked their horns as the bass from nightclubs held the tempo of the city. We passed the airport, every square inch lit up like a summer day. Planes with flashing lights landed and took off, timed perfectly. The pinnacle of punctuality…sometimes.

Judging from the map I studied in the bus station, the road I wanted was just ahead so I reached up and pulled the cord and with a bell chime, the bus pulled over and the door slid open to a darkened street.

I stepped off, and the bus pulled away, leaving me alone in what appeared to be an industrial area. There were giant warehouses with tall fences topped with barbed wire. I walked along the dark street until I found the address I was looking for.

A short chain and padlock held the gates securely closed, but I wiggled through between them and got to the other side without having to mess with the barbed wire. I moved to the shadows of the building and walked along the wall, listening for movement or voices. When I got to the back corner, I heard a slow heartbeat inside. It was too slow and fluttery. It could be a vampire, but I was willing to bet it was Ben.

I found a back door. It was locked, and I didn't know if there were any vampires inside, but I took off my jacket and wrapped my hand in it and then punched the safety glass in the industrial door. It shattered into glass pebbles and made a ton of noise. Any vampire would have heard that. I didn't wait though. I unlocked the door and stepped into the dark warehouse. It was a vast empty space, but to my right was a rickety staircase that led up. The weak heartbeat was coming from up there.

Climbing the stairs, I found another locked door at the top, this one was solid wood, but had a simple lock. I kicked it and it swung open, revealing a dark office space and a bloody gawky Ben, tied to a chair.

On a steel office desk sat his laptop. It was open but set to the lock screen. I flipped it closed and turned to look at the pathetic kid. His chin was resting on his chest and he had several bite marks. The bites left weeping, oozed rivulets down his neck to disappear beneath his black t-shirt.

Little idiot.

I grabbed a box cutter from the desk and sliced the ropes that held him. He tipped forward and nearly landed on his head, but I caught him and hefted him over my shoulder.

I hadn't seen his security password for his laptop yet. I needed him if I wanted to complete my work.

As I reached the bottom of the stairs, the hairs on the back of my neck rose. I was being stalked. I turned and left the warehouse. Fully aware I had been seen. They already knew who I was. Why they weren't attacking I had no idea, but I just kept moving until I got to the gate. I set Ben on the ground, and slid through the gate, with the laptop. Then reached back through and dragged Ben behind me.

I was almost back to the bus stop and wondering how I would get his bloody passed-out ass onto the city bus, when flashing lights and sirens of four police cars came flying up and slammed on their brakes, surrounding me.

The cops got out, crouching in the doors of their vehicles, and pointed their guns at me. They screamed to drop the person. Sounded painful for Ben, but I followed their instructions.

SIXTEEN

"Sorry," I whispered to him when he thumped to the ground and groaned. Seemed the bump might have woke him.

"Get on the ground!" the officer shouted.

"I saved him. You should point your guns at that warehouse!" I yelled back.

They kept yelling at me, so I finally lay down and let them put their stupid flimsy cuffs on me. They still hadn't realized I was a vampire. Apparently, they thought a woman could carry all hundred and fifty pounds of awkward teenage Ben. They would have a surprise when they got me to the police station.

An ambulance came roaring up as the officer pushed me into the back of the police car, then got in the passenger seat. Another officer slid behind the wheel and pulled away from the scene.

"You better protect that kid. They will come back for him."

"Shut it." The officer behind the wheel said as he drove through the city.

I leaned back awkwardly on my cuffed hands. Bunch of idiots. Maybe if I kept my mouth shut, they would release me and no one needed to find out about this.

At the station, they pulled into an underground garage similar to the one in my old hometown. They got out and one of them spoke on the phone for a few minutes before the other one opened the door and hauled me out, smashing my head off the car door frame.

"Did you do that to that boy? Are you a vampire?" he asked. I guess the word had gotten out about Ben's condition.

I kept my mouth shut as suggested.

"It doesn't matter, the master of the city will be here soon. You can explain it to him and the Blood Guard."

Great. I needed to figure out my story before Matthew arrived. The officers led me to a cell to wait for him and the Blood Guard.

I didn't have long to wait. Not long enough to come up with something believable to tell Matthew. So, when they moved me into an interrogation room where Matthew stood, arms crossed, back leaning against the wall and a scowl on his face, I chose silence.

The door shut behind the officer and the room mocked my silence. Matthew was perfectly still. Not a rustle or inhale. I trained my eyes on the table in front of me. The hair on my neck rose. He was stalking me. I could feel his eyes trace my features like he was trying to find a way into my head.

"I have spoken for you," he said, breaking our standoff.

All the air rushed out of my lungs like a collapsing balloon.

"They have released you to me."

I wanted to stand and leave, but he was still leaning against the wall. I kept my eyes trained on the table in front of me, Matthew in my peripheral vision. "I want you to speak to someone. A friend of mine." I raised my eyes to meet his.

"You will do this or I will send you back to live with your father."

He hadn't held my father over my head before now. Nodding silently, I expected it, but the betrayal still pinched. I had done nothing wrong but was being punished anyway.

I would have preferred gardening.

Matthew pushed off the wall and said: "Come on."

I followed him through the police station to his Corolla waiting in the parking lot.

I slipped into the passenger seat and Matthew took us home.

When he parked in the underground lot and killed the engine, I went to get out, but Matthew grabbed my arm. I stopped but didn't look at him.

"Did you bite that boy?" he asked.

I shook my head.

He reached over and turned my face so I was looking at him. "Did you bite that boy?" He asked again, looking into my eyes.

"No, Matthew. I did not bite that boy," I said, holding his glare.

"Thank you, Ren."

The irony of asking me to tell the truth while using my fake name was not lost on me. I just didn't feel much like laughing.

"You are to stay in the Casino unless escorted."

I rolled my eyes.

"Do you understand?" he asked.

"Yes," I replied with no inflection.

He released my arm and exited the vehicle. I followed him to the lobby where he pushed the button on the elevator.

"Good night," he said as he turned and walked to the door that led to the back halls of the casino. He stopped and waited there as I got on the elevator. As the doors closed, he disappeared from view and I went up to the top floor, alone.

I wondered if the police saved Ben's laptop.

SEVENTEEN

The next few days dragged by. When I wasn't working, I stayed in my suite, but by Wednesday night I was ready to bust out. I squished myself into a tiny dress and put on some strappy heels.

Matthew had sent word, through Thor, that he would pick me up and take me out to dine tonight. Matthew himself had been avoiding me. Or maybe he was just busy.

There was a knock on my door promptly at 9pm, and I opened it to find Matthew standing before me in well-fitted jeans and a thin black v neck t-shirt. His wide chest and sculpted abs were on display and I couldn't help but look. He got a crooked grin when he noticed, but it didn't stop me from looking. It's not like his soft blue eyes didn't rake over my tiny dress and everything it didn't cover, too.

"Hey," I said.

"Hey," he replied. "You ready to go?"

"Yup." This wasn't awkward at all.

We took the elevator down to the parking garage, but he didn't lead me to the Corolla. Instead, he ushered me over to a cherry red, 1968 Mustang convertible. Its glossy paint sparkled in the garage's lighting.

"Holy crap, Matthew. Where has this been hiding?" I asked him.

He laughed. "I keep it in a private garage. Some people who frequent casinos can't park and I don't like scratches and dents."

He put the roof down and I tied up my hair with an elastic from my purse. I wouldn't be able to entice my prey tonight with crazy wind-blown hair.

The city was stunning from the passenger seat of a powerful car. The engine ripped through the night, and the feeling of freedom rushed in with the wind. Lights of the Strip twinkled off the hood, and I closed my eyes, letting the night take me away.

"What are you thinking?" Matthew asked.

"Nothing," I replied.

"Nothing?"

"No, Matthew. I'm not thinking anything. I feel like life doesn't get better than this."

"How do you know?"

"How do I know what?" I asked, opening my eyes and studying his profile as he steered the car to wherever we were going.

"How do you know it's the best there is?"

"Because I've been living for 200 years and nothing compares to the feeling of a fast car and an open road." "Have you been living?" That was definitely his psychiatrist's voice.

"What do you mean? Of course, I've been living. I mean, we're dead, right? But that doesn't seem to stop me from going about my business," I replied.

"Hmm," he replied, cryptically. I considered his words for several minutes, my eyes studying his profile.

He rolled up to a high-end nightclub and smiled at me before getting out. His smile stopped the whole conversation, and I felt the usual flush of adrenaline the prospect of hunting brought. The nightclub music was deep and fast and I could already smell the hot writhing bodies that would be inside. I stepped out of the car and Matthew took my hand, wrapping it around his arm. We walked into the nightclub queen and king of the night and I wondered if maybe this was the best feeling in the world for him. Vampires loved power and prey.

We were top of the food chain and on the prowl.

We walked to the bar where Matthew ordered us drinks and I scanned the club. It was at least twice the size of any club I had been to. The DJ was on a stage at the opposite end of the space, pumping out loud, throbbing music, and between him and us, was a sea of young, healthy victims moving to the beat.

My skin prickled, and I looked at Matthew to find he was studying me. There would be no talking in here, the music was too loud. I smiled at him and downed my drink, then walked into the fray, leaving him behind. I danced. The lights and sounds consumed me.

The scent of warm bodies perked my appetite and drove my hunting instincts wild.

Matthew's gaze followed me as if he was hunting me and it pushed my adrenaline higher. My teeth itched to break skin and my stomach clenched in anticipation. The room was spinning with beautiful people; I only had to choose one and they would be mine.

I let my eyes scan until I saw what I wanted. A young man, dancing with a young woman. They looked like a couple. The all-American couple. The man was fit, with enough muscle to fill out his t-shirt, and the young woman was slim with long hair and legs to match. Perfectly feminine. They could have easily graced the cover of a magazine as they moved together.

He was perfect the prey. He was tall and his hair was long enough I could run my fingers through it.

I danced in their direction slowly, extending the hunt for my own pleasure. The young woman's eyes lit upon me once and I ducked behind a tall man. When I stepped back out, her eyes had moved back to her lover.

I moved more stealthily, in a curving line so she wouldn't spot me. My neck prickled again but I didn't like the distraction this time. I focused on my prey. Why hadn't Matthew found his own? That's when I saw him. Behind the long-haired girl. He was dancing there, just behind her. His eyes were on mine like he was waiting for me to catch up. Or daring me too.

I stepped in behind my victim and my eyes locked on the woman. I flashed my fangs at her and she tipped her head, baring her neck. Matthew did the same and my prey tipped his head too. It was a perfect moment when the room stopped. I wrapped my arms around my target from behind and I slid my teeth into his neck. He was nearly too tall for me to reach this way, but when his knees gave out, I held him and pulled the metallic blood into my mouth. His heart forced more blood out of his body and into mine. Matthew's soft blue eyes found mine as he held his victim. His forearm muscles bulged below her breasts in a shattering contrast. His sharp hard lines against her soft curves.

I closed my eyes for a moment, relishing the life that struggled to permeate my body. The fleeting sense I, too, was living. When I opened my eyes again, Matthew was still watching me.

My heart's first beat shook my chest like an old engine brought back to life. It stepped into a rhythm faster than the music. I sealed up the wound I had made and steadied my victim on his feet as Matthew did the same.

Matthew released his prey and pulled me into his arms. His mouth fell on mine. The mingling of blood blossomed between us like a desert meeting the sea. Our tongues tangled. His heart through his chest raced with mine. The life pushed outward from our centers.

The room crept back into my awareness. Matthew moved me to the music and the rhythm of our hearts. I closed my eyes and tipped my head, satiated and energized. Matthew was right. This was the best feeling on earth. No contest.

He pulled me closer until his mouth was at my ear and he said: "There are more things in heaven and earth..."

The quote floated on my consciousness, just out of reach of my addled mind. I tucked it away to examine later and lost myself in the music and Matthew's arms.

EIGHTEEN

"I told you that you had to talk to someone or I would send you home," Matthew said, playing the card that always worked. We had left the club an hour ago and my heart had stopped beating, making me grumpy. I wanted to go home to my old life, but apparently, I would now talk to some psychiatrist friend of Matthew's.

"Whatever, fine. Jesus." I looked out the window at the freeway. The night had cooled off and Matthew had the top up and the heat on, but it didn't help the cold I felt in my silent chest.

Finally, Matthew pulled off the freeway into a smaller quiet town. It was 4am, and I did not understand what kind of psychiatrist office would be open at this hour, but whatever. I could make this fun.

When the car parked in front of an office building, Matthew cut the engine and got out. My door opened a second later.

"Let's go."

"I was coming. You don't have to hold my hand."

He took my hand anyway. I rolled my eyes, but he walked me through the front doors and into the elevator.

I tried to take my hand back, but he tucked it under his arm and rested his palm on the back of my hand where it lay on his forearm.

When the doors opened again, we were in a hall full of offices with plaques on the doors. We stopped at the door that read 'Dr. E P Mallard Ph.D.' "I'm seeing a duck?" I asked.

"Don't be a jerk," he muttered.

I chuckled, and he scowled at me. "By the way, that boy you saved survived." The smile fell off my face.

"The doctors said if he lost much more blood he would have died."

I tried to pull my arm away from him but he gripped it tighter and pulled me through the doorway.

"You saved his life," he said.

"Shut up. Let go of me," I said, struggling to get away from him.

"Hello, Matthew. It's nice to see you," said a woman dressed in a skirt suit. She looked mid-40s with a few grey hairs starting and was a human.

"Emily, very good to see you too. I'd like to introduce you to Ren." He let go of my hand and I almost fell over I had been pulling so hard when he let go.

"Hello, Ren. I've heard so much about you." The woman said, ignoring my near collision with the floor.

I glared at Matthew and mumbled, "Believe none of what you hear and only half what you see."

She laughed, a light tinkle of a sound that made me hate her and like her all at once.

"Come on in, we can have a chat," she said, walking through a door into an office and leaving me to follow. I watched her sit down in a chair across from a small couch. Behind me, Matthew sat in a plastic chair beside the door we had come in, like a bouncer. It was a trap. I couldn't go back and I didn't want to go forward. I thought about making a break for it. The clock on the wall ticked the seconds like it was mocking me. I could just run. Leave Las Vegas and keep running. I could hide from the murderous bastard that had ruined my life.

Payday wasn't till Friday though. I would need to find a computer to get money in my account so I could get out of town.

I tried to think of anyone who would help me, but no one came to mind.

"You coming?" Emily asked.

Shit. I took a deep breath and walked into the room, closing the door behind me.

I walked over and sat on the couch. My leg bounced, and I dug my nails into my thigh to make it stop.

"Why don't you tell me a bit about yourself?" she asked.

I looked back at the door.

"The room is soundproof. He can't hear you, but I do have a call button here." She showed me a small device in her hand.

"Are you afraid of me?" I asked.

"Not at all, but it's good to have a link to the outside world if we need it."

Lie. She thought I would eat her. I smiled, showing off my fangs and her heart rate ticked up a notch.

"All right, here is the deal. Matthew asked me to help you. I don't typically talk to vampires, but I have spent my life with a vampire. I know what you just did and you can keep pushing or you can just talk for a little while and then Matthew will take you home. He will bring you here twice a week either way."

I crossed my arms over my chest.

"Good, so tell me what you did today," she said.

That seemed reasonably simple. "I went to work, then dined with Matthew and then came here." "How was work?" she asked.

"It was boring. I dealt cards for eight hours."

"What would you rather have been doing?"

"I don't know," I said picking at the polish on my thumbnail.

She sat in silence for a minute. I thought about Ben's laptop. I could have taken all that money from the loser and given it back to sick kids. Maybe Ben would come back to the casino.

"What are you thinking about right now?"

"Nothing,", I said, snapping back to the room.

"Ok, so that nothing you were just thinking about was something important to you if you don't want to talk about it. You don't have to tell me, but I promise if you did, I wouldn't share it with anyone else. That is what I'm here for. You can tell me things and I won't tell anyone."

I laughed. "Like a priest?"

"Exactly like that."

I stared at her for a moment, trying to judge if she was lying. She sounded truthful.

I played with the idea. She didn't look like a priest and we weren't in a church. I glanced back at the door.

"I won't tell him either. He knows the rules, he won't even ask," she said like she had read my mind.

"Is it a sin if you are just righting the wrong?" I asked.

She shook her head. "I don't judge you, Ren."

"My name is Nia. Lavinia."

Her eyes went wide. If she was part of the vampire community, she would know who I am.

"The princess."

"No, I'll never be his princess," I scowled.

"Ok," she said, nodding. "Completely understood. Do you prefer Lavinia?"

"I prefer Nia."

She nodded. "So, you righted a wrong, Nia?"

I still wasn't sure if she would keep her trap shut, but I found confessing to the stupid Elvis unsatisfying. "I hack people who break the law and steal their money."

Her eyebrows shot up before she controlled her features. "And what do you do with the money?" she asked.

"I funnel it through a ton of bank accounts and then divide it up and donate it to whatever charity can use it."

"You keep none of the money?"

"No, it's dirty," I replied.

"Ok," she nodded. "Thank you for sharing that with me."

I nodded. I felt light like I did after talking to Father John.

"Tell me about your father."

Of course, she had to ruin it. "I don't want to talk about him," I said.

"Ok, let's talk about Matthew."

"What about him?"

"What is he like?"

"Are you a Disciple?" I asked. Disciples always asked dumb questions about vampires. They wanted to know all about us like we had the secrets to life.

She smiled and shook her head. "I have known Matthew since I was 5 years old, I would just like to know what you think of Matthew."

"I don't know. He's boring, I guess." The look in his eyes as he drank from the woman earlier in the night splashed across my mind. The words he whispered. "There are greater things in heaven and earth."

"That's from Hamlet."

I guess I said that out loud. "Yes, I know, I'm not uneducated," I retorted.

Her features didn't change but her heart ticked up a bit. I smiled.

"So, you steal from the rich and give to the poor. You are a modern-day Robin Hood?"

"No, I don't do it for the poor. I do it because people, some people, are slimy bastards who feel nothing. When I take their money, they feel something."

"Is your father like that?"

I jumped up. "I told you I didn't want to talk about him."

She leaned back in her chair. Usually, I wanted people to fear me, but the look on her face wasn't fear, she hadn't leaned back because she thought I would hurt her, it was pity. She pitied me. It was like a punch in the gut. I stormed out the door and slammed it behind me.

Matthew stood between me and my escape.

"Move or I will hurt you!" I yelled. His gaze flicked past me and then he stepped out of the way. I slammed through the door and took the stairs to the lobby, then ran out of the building into the early morning. The sun was clawing at the horizon, like a drowning man, fighting to breach the surface.

I ran down the street, my feet slapping hard on the pavement. Matthew didn't chase me, thank God, and when I found a small park with a stream and a bench, I sat down and dropped my head in my hands.

She pitied me. The human with greying hair and sagging skin. The one who would die and rot while I stayed the same.

Red bloody tears streaked my face, and I wiped them away and looked out across the stream. A duck with her ducklings paddled softly on the current. Life flowed through even them. Their tiny hearts pumped their blood much faster than a human's, like a drummer beating inside their tiny bodies.

I stood up to walk out of the park but stopped short when I turned to find Matthew leaning against a tree, watching the ducks too. I knew he saw me, but he didn't look at me. He let me study his features and the way his body leaned casually, but his muscles twitched, giving away his true feelings. He was no more relaxed than I was. He was a bundle of nerves ready to explode into action. I wasn't sure if he was planning to chase me if I ran or if he would run away if I jumped at him.

Instead, I stood still. Did nothing. So we remained like that for longer than was comfortable for either of us. The sun made its way into the world, birthed fully behind Matthew. It poured heat on my skin and burned my eyes as I tried to keep watching the strange vampire before me. More tears ran, this time not in sadness, but in pain from trying to look at the sun. I finally closed my eyes and sank down to the grass. It was damp with the morning dew, but it didn't matter. I pulled my knees to my chest and wrapped my arms around them. Burying my head in my knees, I shut the world away, but for the sound of the tiny ducks quacking and splashing. I retreated farther until there was nothing but blackness. A deep hole I could hide in.

1935

During the Great Depression, nobody had anything, except my father and other rich men. The poor were so poor that they couldn't feed their children and resorted to selling or giving them away to anyone with money. Meanwhile, the rich ate and luxuriated. Many older vampires weathered the storm of the 30s. I did not.

It was during this decade my father began in earnest to have me follow his footsteps to power. I was resistant.

"Please, father!" I begged from behind the locked door.

"You can come out when you are willing to see reason. You are the heir, your place is at my side, leading the community."

"Darling, she is just sowing her wild oats," my mother muttered. She was always the contrast to my father's stern, unyielding temperament.

"It has been a decade. It is time for her to settle down." I listened to his boots as they moved away from the door. He'd had it reinforced with steel. I should have known not to return to this house.

I slumped down to the floor, my head resting against the cold door frame.

"I'm sorry, Nia," my mother whispered. Her voice came through the door at about the same height as I was. I imagined her, leaning against the door opposite me. Her bouncy curls squished on one side as her head rested against mine — one door keeping us apart. What a pair we were.

She stayed with me. We spoke through the door about everything and anything. Day and night, I spent curled on my side, my fingers pressed to the bottom panel of the door where her voice was loudest. I told her about my travels and she told me about novels and poetry. When I grew too weak from lack of blood and my jaw seized, she carried the conversation for both of us. My father tried to get her to come away from the door, but she refused. I knew he would never hurt her. She was his bonded. He couldn't risk losing her since she was half his power as a vampire. When mother stopped speaking, I assumed her jaw had also clenched from lack of blood. There was a jingle of keys and the door swung open.

He had moved her. She was no longer sitting at my door. Shiny shoes stopped in front of my face. I had frozen with my cheek pressed to the carpet, but when blood poured across my lips and sensation returned, I knew my father had folded in our poker game. My mother had won. My freedom was granted. Though he didn't speak to me that day, he fed me enough blood to get me moving and then left my door unlocked.

———

Lifted from the ground, breaking the roots I had thrown down, left me adrift, like a boat, unmoored. Matthew held me to his chest. He was cool but stable — a solid anchor. I tucked my arms into my chest like a child and let him carry me away. He whispered, "Let's go home." Then walked out of the park, me in his arms, and back across town to the parking lot of the psychiatrist's office.

He set me in the front seat and started the car. I closed my eyes and slept till we made it back to the casino, barely rousing when Matthew carried me from the parking garage to the top floor of his hotel. Instead of turning right, he went left and opened the door to his room. His suite was much larger than mine. The décor was antique and classy, like the man himself. I snorted a laugh at my comparison. His blinds were blood red, matching the ones in my suite and his bed, as he laid me down in it, was king size. He pulled the blankets back, and I heard a click as a heated blanket came to life. I curled my knees up to my chest and buried myself in the heat.

"Please stay here. I'll be back," he said.

I did as he asked since I had nowhere else to go.

I slept the day away.

NINETEEN

When I opened my eyes again, it was night. I slid out of the bed and used Matthew's shower, then walked out into the living room and flicked on the TV.

'The Blood Guard took down the notorious vampire and drug king-pin Ed Florence today. The report sent to all media outlets says the Blood Guard caught him killing a human in New York City. He was staked and his body burned in accordance with vampire law. The report did not release the name of the woman he killed, to protect the family.'

"Whoa," I said, flicking off the TV.

I could go home.

I leaned back on the couch. Then stood up and walked out of Matthew's apartment. I took the elevator down and walked the back halls to Matthew's office.

I knocked on the door and then pushed it open. Inside Matthew was sitting on his desk talking to a pretty blonde. She was sitting in his chair, laughing at some witty thing he had said. Just his type. She smiled at me and I narrowed my eyes.

"I'm going home," I told him, then I turned and walked back out of the room, closing the door behind me.

I ran back to the elevator, but I couldn't think of anything I needed from my room, so I went into the casino.

"Carson, I need my pay, I'm leaving," I said when I found the older vampire talking to Thor.

"Where are you going?" he asked.

"Home. I want to leave now. I need my pay so I can get a train ticket back home."

Thor put his finger to his ear and got that far away look in his eyes. "Boss wants to talk to you."

"He looked pretty busy when I was just in there. No need to bother him again," I replied.

"He will have your pay ready if you follow me," Thor said. I shook my head and followed behind the giant vampire. He led me back through the maze, knocked on Matthew's door, then opened it to reveal the office with zero blondes. Only Matthew, sitting behind his desk, pen in hand, looking through some paperwork.

Thor shut the door behind me, leaving us alone. Standing there, I waited. I was as far from Matthew as I could get, contained by the room.

I tapped my fingers on my thigh, impatience wearing me down. "Do you have my pay?" I asked.

He lifted his head and looked at me. "You don't have to leave."

"Yes, I do. This isn't my life."

"It could be."

"Dealing Black Jack isn't a life."

"You could do something else. I want you to stay."

I stared at him. There was no reason he wanted me to stay.

"I already have a life in Belcrest."

"Stealing from rich people and watching soap operas isn't a life."

"I knew that bitch couldn't keep her mouth shut!" I yelled.

"It wasn't Emily. It was the deaf boy you saved. He spilled it all when I told him I would kill you for hurting him. Seems you've made a loyal friend."

"He is just a kid. He doesn't even know what he's talking about."

"Too late, you already admitted to telling Emily you stole from wealthy scum bags." I glared at him.

He nodded. "Ok, fine. Here is your check. You can spend it on a train ticket or whatever you want. But you have a place here, and friends."

I walked across the room and took the check from his hand, stuffed it in my pocket and then walked back across the room and out the door without another word, slamming it hard behind me.

As I marched through the lobby, a loud clap from behind me made me turn my head.

Ben stood there with a pen and paper, scribbling.

I turned back to walk out, but the boy caught up and grabbed my arm.

I hissed at him, but he didn't back down. He held up the paper. It said, "Please don't go."

"How do you even know I'm leaving?"

His pen scratched over the paper again before he held it up. "I heard you yelling at Carson."

"You should leave too. Those vampires will come after you again," I said, as I tried to walk away before he could stop me again.

Ben threw his body in front of mine just before I reached the door. I bared my teeth at him like an angry lion. Bold little bugger didn't even bat an eye. I must be getting soft. He just held up one last piece of scribbled paper.

"Matthew killed them. You saved my life. Please stay."

I scoffed and pushed past him. I had saved no one. This kid was worse than a disciple.

I walked out of the Casino and took a bus to the train station. The city rolled by, a blur of colour and lights and music. I walked into the bank beside the train station to deposit the check. When I pulled it out and uncrumpled it, the amount was half a million dollars.

I wasn't sure if it was a joke, but I was sure if I deposited it in the bank machine, I could get enough cash to get home. Ren was dead anyway, I would wish them good luck tracking her down if the check bounced.

The machine spit out 500 dollars and I tucked it in my purse and went across the street to the train station.

"Hi, one ticket to Belcrest please," I asked the lady behind the counter.

"Sure, hon, you going to college there or something?" she asked absent-mindedly as her fingers slammed on the keyboard with her long fake nails.

"Yeah, something like that," I replied

"I have a direct train leaving in the morning, or you can take the next train and do a few transfers. Either way will get you there in about 24 hours."

"I'll take the next train. I want to get going."

"Sure, I totally understand. Vegas isn't for everyone."

I smiled at her and gave her most of the money I had taken out of the bank machine. She handed me the ticket and pointed out the platform for the first of the three trains that would eventually take me home.

The train rolled up to a stop, and I watched all the happy shiny people step off. Groups that were excited to be in Las Vegas; off to gamble and drink too much, party with friends and dance.

I boarded the train and found my seat. I was next to a window, and as the train pulled out of the station, I remembered what the woman at the ticket window had said. Vegas wasn't for everyone. The bright lights and the music. The city that never sleeps. Sin City. It wasn't for everyone.

My mind kept spinning with thoughts of the city, the one I loved. The waves of people. Matthew.

The further I got, the more I wondered where the hell I was going.

My life was in Belcrest, wasn't it?

With a sigh I let it all go. I was going home. I could curl up on my couch and watch soaps under my heated blanket and go to the club on Saturday nights. That was the life I had created for myself and that was what I wanted.

I nodded in and out of sleep, my head on a tiny pillow jammed up against the cold glass of the window. The country flew past, with tall buildings then open fields for miles and miles. I had plenty of time to think about things, but mostly I tried to get the words out of my head. The ones that Matthew had whispered. "There are more things in heaven and earth…"

It was like a puzzle and I wanted to fit the pieces. When I got off the first train, I stopped at a bookstore and bought Hamlet— the Cliff Notes version.

The second train ride was long enough so that I read the Cliff Notes three times.

I kept getting stuck on the quote. It didn't make sense. I needed the full version of the book. The next train transfer was too quick, and I didn't have time to find a bookstore. I would have to wait until I got home.

On the last leg of my trip, I tried to nap, but my mind wouldn't shut up. The man in the seat next to me he had a laptop out and was surfing the net.

"Hi," I said.

He looked up and smiled. "Hey, how's it going?" He had a New York accent. It was kind of dirty and delicious.

"Not bad. Where are you headed?"

"Nowhere. I bought a pass and I'm seeing the country," he replied.

"You are going nowhere?"

"Yup, wherever the train takes me."

"How will you know when you reach the end?" I asked, turning in towards him.

"Wherever I am when the clock strikes midnight on January first, that is the end."

"Then what?"

"Well, I guess I get a job and find a place to stay and start a life," he said with a shrug.

"Are you a vampire?" I asked. Vampires would change place and names and start over when they got bored. I'd never heard of a human doing it.

"No," he laughed. "Just trying to find my place in the world, and maybe fate will have better luck than I have."

I sat back in my seat and pondered fate. It was the opposite of religion. Fate wasn't a father's guiding hand, it was more like a practical joke. Perfectly set up with cause and effect.

"Where are you headed?" he asked, breaking me out of my thoughts.

"I don't know anymore," I replied.

He nodded, knowingly, like we were kindred spirits.

When I got off the train in Belcrest, I was the only person in the station except for the janitor who ran his mop left and right across the tiled floor. I exited the station and walked through town to my apartment. It was a good hour by foot, but I had no one waiting for me and had been sitting so long, my legs had gotten stiff.

It was Friday night and there were lots of college students around town. They were all filled with youthful enthusiasm; their laughter and calls echoed through the moonlit streets of my little city. I wanted to join them.

Go dancing and feel their life pressed up against me, but the city held no pleasure for me right now. I got back to my old building and realized I didn't even have my keys. I called up to Mrs. Henderson's apartment, but she didn't answer. Probably going deaf.

Finally, I sat down on the steps and rested my head against the hard brick exterior of the apartment building. I stayed there until morning when a police car rolled up and parked in front of me.

"Hey, Bert, how's it going?" I said as his bushy eyebrows came together, though my voice made the question sound tired and I wondered if the joke was getting old.

"I brought your keys for your new door. Mrs. Henderson had your spare set, so I brought them too."

"Where is Mrs. Henderson?" I asked as I stood up and dusted my pants off.

"She passed away."

I froze and raised my eyes to meet Jenkins'. "She died?"

"Yeah, last week," he replied, holding out my keys.

She was really old but for some reason, I didn't think she would ever actually die. With 19 grandchildren and some great-grandchildren running around, she had more life in her pinky finger than I had in my whole body.

I took the keys. "Thanks, Jenkins." I turned and walked into the building. Then I took the elevator up to my apartment and unlocked the door. I paused in the doorway and listened, straining my ears to hear Mrs. Henderson's heartbeat. I knew in my mind she was dead, but the sound of her heart was so much a part of the building, I imagined it would just keep thumping. It was silent. Snuffed out like a candle in the wind.

I shut the door behind me and turned the lock. My apartment was still a mess from the idiot with the stakes, but at least my door had been fixed. I crawled into my bed and flicked on my old heated blanket. It felt good to lie down after 24 hours of sitting and I spent the next day sleeping.

TWENTY

Saturday night, I got up and showered. I found a cute skirt and paired it with a tank top. Then I swept my hair up into a high ponytail so it swung around my shoulders. I called a cab and grabbed my purse.

I paused at Mrs. Henderson's door again. It was still silent. I wondered how long it would take for someone new to move in. Hopefully, they wouldn't have children.

I took the elevator down and stepped out onto the street. It was cool and damp here, something I had forgotten. The desert air was dry in Las Vegas. I missed that.

My heels clicked on the sidewalk and I slid into the waiting cab. I watched the quiet city slip past. It was dark and sleepy.

When the cab stopped in front of Ray's, I walked past the lineup of college kids and past the bouncer who held the door for me. Inside the music pounded. I slipped onto a bar stool.

"Nia!" Ray called. "Where you been?"

"Nowhere!" I shouted back.

He shook his head and got me a drink. I downed it fast, and he handed me another. The second one went down just as fast and I felt like my old self again. I got up and danced with a group of barely legal kids. They were drunk. The girls were holding hands and laughing while the guys were trying to dance with them. They were all stupid, but I tried to ignore it and dance. If I got lost in the music, I could get back in the swing of things. I half-heartedly scanned the room for a target but saw no one I wanted.

After polishing off another drink, I headed back out to the dance floor when the hair on the back of my neck prickled. I spun around and scanned the crowd. He couldn't be here. I saw no one, but I was definitely being hunted. My adrenaline spiked. I danced, glancing around, trying to find the hunter that stalked me.

———

For hours someone hunted me but whoever it was avoided my line of sight, driving me crazy. Frustrated, I turned to the closest human and bared my fangs, sinking them into his neck the same moment he tipped his head. I bit hard and drank fast before sealing his wound and storming through the crowd to escape. As I moved farther away from the club, the music hushed and the city surrounded me with its sleepy darkness.

The pre-dawn dew fell on my bare shoulders as my heart beat pounded an angry song in my chest. The feeling wasn't euphoric, it was antagonizing like the eyes that stalked me all night. I had never even glimpsed the vampire who hunted me. It could have been Ryan though it wasn't his style. He preferred me to look at him like he was a peacock and his colourful tail would win me over.

I climbed the stairs to my apartment as my heart slowed and closed my door behind me to the final beat. Blocking out the night with the click of my lock, I let the idea it could have been Matthew die with the last of my conscious thoughts. Sleep took me away.

———

The next evening, I went back to the club. My mind wouldn't let go of the thought it had been Matthew watching me. I had to prove it wrong. I sat on a bar stool and drank. I thought I felt someone watching me once, but I couldn't see anyone and I never felt it again. I prayed all night it would be Ryan, acting strange, but he didn't show up either. I was the only vampire in the bar full of humans. Eventually, I grew tired and went home.

As I walked in the door, I reached for the lights, but a steel arm wrapped around my waist and something sharp stabbed at my neck, sending ice through my veins. The world went black.

"Good morning, Princess," a voice I didn't recognize said.

"I'm not a princess," I muttered. The masculine voice chuckled. Who the hell was in my room? Sensation returned to my body and I felt heavy iron cuffs on my wrists and ankles. I was not in my apartment. I was laying on a cement floor. I moved my arm and the sound of chain clinked. Did they chain me?

I tried to go back through my memory but it was hazy and muddled. I scanned the room. It was a dingy basement or something. The voice was coming from a shadow in the far corner. The gooseflesh on my skin told me he was a vampire. No human had ever made me feel like prey.

"Where am I?" I asked, panic taking over. I pushed my legs to move and stood with a loud clatter of chains. The room was dimly lit with a single bulb. I had about five feet of chain on each of my limbs.

The sound of footsteps above me made me look up at the ceiling and suddenly the vampire from the corner had me pinned. My head cracked off the floor. His fangs sunk deep in my throat, tearing the flesh and grinding off my collar bone as his messy aim and careless bite took away most of the skin of my neck. I screamed and a gurgling sound followed as blood filled my airway. Pulling my legs into my body, I kicked out hard, launching him across the room with a crash.

I jumped to my feet and wrapped a hand around my neck to staunch the flow for the moment it would take for my injury to heal.

The vampire laughed and stepped into the light, my blood smeared on his face. He had long hair and a psychotic glint in his eye.

"What do you want with me?" I croaked when my throat had corrected itself sufficiently.

"Me? I want nothing with you. Although you taste delicious." He laughed and walked out, closing the door behind him. His shoes clomped on the stairs. I strained my ears to listen but murmured voices and feet shuffling was all I heard. A door opened upstairs and another set of feet added to the murmurs. I slid down the cement wall and sat on the floor. I had to shuffle my chains, but I wrapped my arms around my knees and waited.

A few hours later, I stood up to stretch and my legs were already tight. I hadn't lost much blood, but it was enough I would probably freeze up if I stayed down here much longer.

I didn't want to make too much noise, but I wrapped one chain around my hand and pulled hard, hoping the ring they attached it to would break out of the cement. It didn't budge. If I had just had a blood meal, I could have done it but I hadn't eaten last night and, bitten by that disgusting vampire, I didn't have the strength.

"That won't work, Nia." That voice I recognized.

I turned and hissed at the bastard, Ryan. I knew he was a total shit.

He dropped his eyes to the floor but didn't move to help me.

"Take the chains off me now, Ryan!" I commanded.

"I can't do that," he replied.

"Do it now!"

"Listen, I tried to win you over, but it didn't work. I need a coven. I can't keep going like this. I might as well die if I'm never have a city."

"You think you will get a city by chaining me in a basement? You will get your head on a pike!"

"You don't know the old laws. Before the awakening, there was a law that said if a vampire possessed the heir, they would get the dowry."

"Possessed?" I scoffed. "I don't think it meant chaining her up."

"That's exactly what it meant." He sneered. "You weren't around when every move you made was part of a game of chess. Back then vampires didn't drink from peasants. They drank from human kings and queens and owned the city they controlled. Time changed everything! Now there are no kings and queens and your father controls all the cities on this continent. How am I supposed to get ahead when he chooses who will succeed and who will get the scrapings left behind?"

"So that's it then?" I asked. "You'll keep me locked away so you can have a city? What will happen once you have this dowry you believe you are entitled too?"

"You will stay with me forever, Nia." His voice lowered, his eyes just barely reaching mine. "Either by will or by force."

"It will never be by choice." He nodded and turned to leave.

"Where are you going?"

He kept walking, closing the door behind him. I slid down to the floor again. Cold and exhausted. Stupid vampires and their idiotic laws. It would have been nice to know about this particular one before now. I could have protected myself from desperate idiots like Ryan.

There were no windows in the room they chained me in, so I lost track of time. Eventually, I stopped moving, my joints seized, my jaw stuck shut. My eyes blinked, but my eyelids felt like sandpaper as they ran over my eyeballs. I would mummify next. My consciousness would stay intact, but my body would dry until I was leathery skin over bone. I had seized with my knees pulled up to my chest. Like an infant curled in sleep, and just as vulnerable.

The time passed, I assumed. My mind would drift in and out.

At one point I drifted in as there were people standing around me. Ryan's face came into view, but my eyes couldn't track him.

"We are going to our new city," he said, as he slipped from view.

"God, this is disgusting. Remind me never to skip a meal." A voice I would never forget said. It was the vampire who had bitten me. When I had my chance, I would stake him and burn his body to ash.

My hands and feet had no sensation at all, but as they lifted me a hollow, mournful sound came from my throat. My legs were being forced to move by their careless treatment and it felt like knives stabbing my knees.

"Now, now. None of that. We need to get to our new home, maybe then you can have a little drink to feel better, hmm?" I felt the rumble of his words. The vampire who bit me was carrying me now.

"Cecil, you shouldn't provoke her," Ryan said.

Now I had a name to for the vampire I would slaughter. He would die painfully. I would make sure. Ryan would die too. I would spare no vampire who was part of this.

My vengeance would paint the walls red.

TWENTY-ONE

We travelled for a long time. I was under a blanket on the back seat of a car. It was pitch black and I couldn't tell if my eyelids had stopped blinking. If so, it was only a matter of time before my vision left me.

There was no way I could save myself now. I sunk into my sadness like it was a soft bed. My tired mind let go of the present and didn't rouse itself again until I heard a clatter. It was the sound of sliding jail door. That hollow steel sound was like the police station jail, but I could see enough out of one eye to tell I was not in Jenkins' jail. I was somewhere dark and damp.

They must have carried me in here, but I had slept through it. At least that meant I no longer felt pain. I wasn't a glass half full person, but this was a different circumstance.

"I have my city, now, Nia." Ryan's voice rang in the space like an empty concert hall. "I will give you more time to think about things. But I hope you will join me and help me run the city. Baltimore could use a princess."

I couldn't be further from Las Vegas now without leaving the country. Baltimore. My father must have been laughing when he sent me here. They get snow in the winter. They could even have snow now. It must be close to Christmas. Or perhaps Christmas had passed. Time didn't matter anymore.

Ryan's face came into view and then moved too far and all I could see was his neck. "Please, think about it, Nia." His hand came up close to my face. He must have moved my hair back. I couldn't feel anything now. "You are so beautiful, it seems a crime to leave you like this."

But he walked out anyway, leaving me to my desperation.

I craved blood for days. My mind, broken. I could smell the copper tang and feel skin on my tongue. I swore there was blood near me, but I was blind now. There could be a pot of fresh blood in front of me and I would still starve and waste away here. For weeks or months, I languished in the dark silence — broken only by a constant drip. I counted 27 seconds between the drips. I could almost see it there, a tiny drop of water hanging on the brim of a tap, building and building until its weight bore it to the ground. Drip.

Drip.

Drip.

I counted them. The rhythm they created was almost pleasant. My mind convinced me it was a heartbeat. That someone was standing before me with a pulse. A vampire or a human. I hoped it was a human. The tiny heartbeat was pushing blood through a body, not releasing water from a tap.

The jail cell door slid open one day while I was counting the heartbeats or the water drips. I had made it over a million, but I had slept sometimes in between. Missing out on those heartbeats or water drips drove me to stay awake longer. I kept counting.

"I'm sorry, Nia. I wish I could release you." Ryan's voice was drowning out the heartbeats. I wanted him to shut up. "This city is a mess and I'm afraid I can't risk you. Someday soon I will make sure you come back, but for now, you must stay safe." His voice sounded unsure. He had no business running a city. Soon someone would kill him and take over. Although I doubt many vampires wanted Baltimore.

"Your friend Matthew has been troublesome," his voice was closer now. Right above me. "He's powerful and old. I didn't think anyone but your mother would want you back." Now he sounded scared. Matthew had Las Vegas on the other side of the country, what he would want with Baltimore?

"I'll be back in a few years. Seeing you like this is upsetting. Perhaps by then, the city will be under control and Matthew will have given up."

I wanted to laugh. A few years. What's a few years when you lived for centuries or millennia. My body wouldn't get any weaker now. I was at the lowest a vampire could get. As long as no one staked me I would go on indefinitely.

And so I did.

Locked in my tomb. I counted heartbeats and imagined the lights of Las Vegas. The city that never sleeps. Sin City.

I remembered Matthew's soft blue eyes but tried not to think about blood or nightclubs. I thought of Matthew behind his desk, watching me with appraising eyes. The smile on his face the last time I saw him. It wasn't a smile for me, it was for a blonde woman, but he was so beautiful when he smiled.

"Nia." It was Matthew's voice.

"I'm down here!" I screamed.

"Nia, where are you?"

"I'm down here, trapped in this cell!" I banged on the bars.

"Are you down there, Nia?" The voice faded away.

"Please! I'm down here. Don't go!"

—

Drip.

What a cruel dream.

I was dead, for all intents and purposes, but I was not really dead because I still dreamed. I still heard the metronome of my existence. Drip.

My mind replayed my mother's soft voice, singing a beautiful French opera. I could smell her candy scent and see her loving eyes in my mind.

"Come sing with me, Lavinia," my mother said. The sun came in through the window in the parlour. Father was drinking a glass of wine and reading a book. Half listening to mother sing.

"You know I don't like to sing, Mother," I said, sitting beside her at the piano.

"But you have such a beautiful voice. Let me hear you sing," she begged.

"All right," I sighed.

I sang her several of the songs she had taught me, in French. She smiled the whole time and clapped her hands after each song before begging for one more. She was an angel.

———

I controlled my mind and tried not to let it stray to my father when I was awake. He knew where I was, but still, I lay here, in this prison that my body had become. Matthew knew too. Baltimore. But when I fell asleep, my dreams would haunt me.

———

I walked into the parlour where my father was reading the newspaper, dressed in his finest clothes and my mother was fussing over a bouquet.

"Lavinia, why are you not dressed?" my father asked. He expected me in a white dress, my hair pinned and veil lowered. Ready to make a union of his design. Instead, I wore loose-fitting navy blue pants and a formfitting shirt. The style worked for my figure and my temperament.

It was the 1940s now. We were in America during the Second World War. Women were taking their lives as their own and no longer living to serve men. My father didn't care for the decade or the direction it was taking.

"I don't want to marry him, father."

"I don't care what you want. You will be an ideal pair. Powerful enough to take over some day," His ire was growing, but I didn't care. My mother's worried face wouldn't stop the road I was travelling down this time. I had grown too large to fit in the small box my father wanted to keep me in. My heart longed to escape the oppression and my mind finally gave me the way.

"I don't want to take over and the vampire is cruel. He is not who I would want to spend my life with. He is cowardly and foolish," I said.

My father's hand struck out so fast, I didn't see it coming. I hit the far wall with a crunch and slid to the floor.

"Oh no!" my mother cried, but she did not rush to my side like she did when I fell off my pony. I had put her in between my father and me all these years. Her heart didn't know what to do when he and I fought. The time had come for me to make the choice for her.

I righted myself and popped my shoulder back into the socket. I looked at my father with the broken jaw he had given me and pulled the bone back into place with a crunch. Anger infused my veins and gave me a backbone that day. I gathered a few of my things and walked out the front door to the sound of my mother crying. My father didn't look up from his newspaper.

I supposed Baltimore was a big place. Drip. 3,645, 292.

If my father was looking for me, he might have trouble finding me in a big city. Not that I thought he was looking for me. Besides, if he found me, he might just tuck me away like this for safe keeping too. Drip. 3,645,293.

There was a yell. Or maybe my mind made it up. I thought of Matthew's soft blue eyes for the thousandth time or maybe the millionth time. Who was counting? His soft blue eyes though. So warm and hungry.

"This way," Matthew's voice said.

I didn't remember him saying that. Maybe when he led me to his office one time.

"She is down here somewhere. Find her!" he yelled.

I didn't remember him saying that before either. My memory was slipping.

"Holy shit, what is that?"

That sounded like Thor. Was I still dreaming?

The sound of the jail cell door sliding open lit on my ears. I dared not hope. I was sure it was a trick of my mind. I couldn't let myself hope the door had opened. But the stomping of boots on cement drowned out the next drip.

"Hello, Ren. Nia." Matthew breathed. His voice was so close now, I wasn't sure I could keep denying he was here. I didn't want to give in to the mind tricks, but if he was really here…

"Are you sure that's her?" Thor asked.

"Yes, it's her. Let's get her home," Matthew said. I wanted to cry. I felt nothing, but Matthew said: "I've got you now." Right in my ear. His lips couldn't have been more than a few inches away. If I had the ability, I would have cried. I pleaded for my eyes to spring a tear. The pressure was so intense I could hardly take it.

"I've staked Ryan and his guards. You know that means I'm the lord of freaking Baltimore now. I had no interest in Baltimore, Nia," Matthew whispered in my ear. He continued talking close to me until he must have set me down. I heard him talking from a little further away. A car engine started.

"I'm going to pick up some blood for you, Nia. I don't think you are in any condition to hunt today. I have the heat on full. You will be fine soon." The car engine roared.

We were moving away from my prison. I let myself believe it even though I couldn't be sure. If this was an elaborate dream, I wanted to stay in it forever.

"I'll be right back," Matthew said as the engine died. "Thor is here, Nia. He will guard you." A door opened and closed and then it was silent again for a minute.

"He damn near burned the city to the ground for you, little vampire girl," Thor's voice was gravelly. "Don't make me regret helping him. You broke his heart once, I won't see it broken again."

The words were hushed, but they reached my ears. It was possibly the most the vampire security guard had ever spoken in my presence. His words sunk into me and I toyed with them until I heard the car door open again.

"Let's get her somewhere safe first. I got her six pints. Hopefully, that will be enough to bring her back." His voice carried to my ears as though he were looking at me. I felt self-conscious now. I had never seen a vampire emaciated in person, but I had seen photos. I imagined my face sunken, lips pulled back, baring my incisors like a rabid dog.

The sound of the tires on the pavement lulled me and I dozed off and on. When the car stopped again, I heard the door open closest to me.

"All right, Nia. Let's get you back, huh?" Matthew said, his voice close to my ear again. I assumed he was carrying me, and I wanted to feel his arms around me. I flashed back to the night at the club when he danced with me. When he held me, his lips at my ear as he quoted Hamlet, of all things.

It clicked together. I knew what he meant that night. I was so stupid.

"Here you go, Nia."

I felt my tongue first. It stung with sensation. My throat burned like I was drinking fire. My jaw moved for the first time in a long time with a pop and I chocked on the blood.

"You're ok, Nia. Give it a minute." My teeth clicked several times of their own free will. Like a set of wind up teeth on a table top. Click. Click. click. Then they latched onto a blood bag. And my throat pulled hard, dragging the thick blood into my shriveled stomach. My face flushed and my eyes pricked as bloody tears rolled down towards my ears. I could feel I was lying on a bed now. My arm moved, and no chains clicked. I tried to move my arms deliberately towards my face, but instead, they flew up and connected with Matthew. Vision returned to one eye. Everything was blurry, but I tried to track Matthew as he avoided my arms swinging out of control.

When he caught them, he tucked them in under the blanket. Then his weight settled beside me on the bed. Tears tickled my face as they soaked down into my hair. I blinked, and the universe came into focus.

"There you are," Matthew said, smiling down at me like an angel from heaven. I thought I wasn't remembering his eyes properly in my dreams, but here, now, they were the exact colour of the summer sky; endless and vast. They twinkled at me as I soaked in his features. His beautiful lips pulled back in a smile wide enough to show his teeth.

I blinked again.

'You ready for more?" he asked.

I opened my mouth, but no sound came out. I tried again, but then another blood bag was in front of my mouth and I bit down. The moan that came from my throat was dry and sounded tortured even though the ecstasy made my eyes roll back in my head. I eagerly sucked the blood from the bag now though my stomach felt distended.

When it was empty, my whole body began to shake, my teeth chattered, and I tried to move my legs. They were still up by my chest, but I felt a little give in my joints like they might move. I pushed my feet out and screamed as they straightened sending searing pain through my whole lower body. I thrashed and shook while Matthew held me down. More bloody tears ran down my face and I kept screaming until I lost my voice again and then I whimpered and moaned while Matthew smoothed my hair back from my face.

"I'm sorry I took so long to get to you," he whispered into the silence when the pain faded and I stopped writhing. "I promise I will never let you suffer like that again."

I opened my mouth to say something, but I didn't know what to say to him now that he was here, so I closed my mouth again and closed my eyes. Matthew moved off me and tucked in beside me, his body touching mine from foot to shoulder, but he was over the blanket. I realized I was under a heated blanket as the pain dissolved from my lower body and sensation returned. The heat was like a dream too. Hot and dry. I pulled one arm out from under the blanket and slid my fingers into Matthew's hand where it rested on my hip.

He squeezed my hand and held on tight while I drifted off to sleep.

TWENTY-TWO

"Nia, wake up."

"I don't want to," I muttered, pressing my face between the pillows.

"Your voice has returned."

I sat bolt upright. Then rubbed my head which felt dizzy from the abrupt movement. It wasn't a dream.

"Uhm, hi." Matthew stood at the end of the bed, chuckling.

"I need a shower," I said, catching the smell coming from me. It must have been disgusting, sitting so close to me.

"I put some new clothes in there for you."

I pulled back the covers, my arms and legs working fairly well now, though I still felt cold as soon as I slid out from under the heated blanket. Stumbling to the bathroom, I flicked on the shower and glimpsed myself in the mirror. My hair was packed down and dirty. Blood stained my mouth and eyes making me look like a monster. Is that how humans felt as they grew old and their appearance changed? I turned away and stepped into the shower. The hot water was a balm to my frazzled nerves. I squirted a large amount of soap into my hand and tried to wash my hair. It took most of the bottle and a full bottle of conditioner before my hair felt clean. I scrubbed my skin with a loofa until it was red. They had left me to rot for what I calculated to be at least three years in a basement. What's three years?

I sank down in the shower and stayed there until the water ran cold. Then I gathered myself up and shut off the tap. I combed out my hair before I looked in the mirror again. Then, when I looked up, I saw Nia staring back at me. The same as she had always looked. Her eyes bright and hair smooth. She had a wide mouth and a small nose. She had a pair of sharp incisors. She needed to stop referring to herself in the third person.

I slipped on the track pants and hoodie that Matthew had left for me. They were loose and comfortable. When I stepped back out into the hotel room, Matthew smiled at me. The room spun a bit, and I grabbed onto the bathroom door frame for support. In a second, he was by my side, his arm around my waist supporting me.

"Thank you," I whispered. Then I pulled away, standing on my own. "Can we go home?"

"Yes, absolutely. I have a plane waiting to take you back to Belcrest. We can leave now if you like."

I bit my lip and nodded.

Matthew picked up things and stuffed them into bags. He had brought little, but my dirty clothes went into a bag and then into a garbage pail.

"How long was I in there?" I asked.

"In the shower?" he asked, absentmindedly without turning.

"No, not in the shower."

He stopped and sunk down on the bed. "Four years, three months and twenty-two days."

The air left my lungs. That was longer than I had expected.

"Why didn't my father come for me?" I asked and immediately regretted it. "Never mind." I turned away and looked around the room. "Did I have shoes on?"

"Nia," Matthew said my name like a scold. I wasn't a child anymore.

"What?"

"He's not a good example of an old vampire."

I scoffed. "You don't think I know my own father?"

"I think he has tainted your vision of every vampire," he breathed.

"I would agree with you, but another one just let me starve in a basement for four years!" "And now he's dead." "I'm dead, too!" I shouted.

"Not in the way that counts," he said. His voice was calm. It frustrated me.

I laughed unkindly. "What way counts, Matthew? That I am still moving around? How does that count?" I was provoking him and I couldn't stop myself.

"Because if you were really dead, I wouldn't have spent the last four years killing every vampire I got my hands on in bloody Baltimore!" Matthew returned.

I hadn't heard him yell before. It shocked me, snapping me out of my anger.

"Well, I'm sorry to inconvenience you. Next time, I'll try to die more thoroughly," I turned on my heel and locked myself back in the bathroom.

"That's not what I meant, Nia," he shouted through the closed door. I heard something hit the wall, and he swore.

I sat on the floor in front of the counter and tried to calm down, knowing that wasn't what he meant. Why was I like this?

I got up and peeked out the door. Matthew was sitting on the end of the bed, his head in his hands. Why would he spend four years tracking me down? I stepped out of the bathroom and took a step closer to him. He didn't move or look up.

"I'm in love with you, Nia. I have been since the first day you walked into my office and called me on my patriarchal bullshit. Don't make me spend another day without you. I want you in Las Vegas, in my casino. Please, Nia. Don't run away from me." "Why?"

"I told you why," he said.

"No, you told me you love me and want me. Tell me why."

He looked up at me. His eyes brimmed red. "Because you are perfect. You are flawed and beautiful and amazing. You are sinner and saint. You are life and death. You are everything, Nia."

"I'm a mess, Matthew."

"Yes."

"I won't stop being a mess. I'm not a broken doll you can fix."

"I know."

"Ok," I said.

"Ok, what?" Matthew stood up.

"I will come back to Las Vegas with you. But I'm not willing to be some prize on your arm. I'll just come to Vegas."

"Ok," he smiled again and my knees almost crumbled. Matthew Merewin had somehow managed to get under my skin.

We spent the rest of the day and into the night on a plane. Tracing our way back across the country. I slept most of the way, but every time I opened my eyes, Matthew was typing away with the glow of his laptop illuminating his features.

He was a beautiful man. His strong jaw and regal nose were reminiscent of the Vikings of millennia ago. I wondered if he sailed across the seas and pillaged villages. How different his life is now, from those harsh times of kill or be killed.

My mother used to tell me stories. She would try to explain my father. She loved the man I hated most. Her efforts were doomed to fail. But she came from a different time too. When she was young, you chose a man who was harsh because he could protect you and provide for you. A man who was gentle would never keep you or your children alive.

I glanced up at Matthew again. He was gentle but also strong. 'There are more things in heaven and earth, Horatio, than are dreamt of in your philosophy.' He was the thing. The ghost I had seen but hadn't believed. Even the way he had said it was gentle.

I unclipped my seatbelt and moved across the plane. Matthew looked up as I approached, but I kept walking until I was in front of him. I didn't know what I was doing, but he put his laptop aside and pulled me into his lap.

I laughed at how awkward I was, trying to fit in the plane seat with him, but he folded me until I fit perfectly. Then he wrapped his arms around me and held me tight. We sat like that, my ear to his silent chest, his chin resting on top of my head until the pilot came over the speakers and announced we would land soon.

Matthew stood and set me in his seat, buckling my seatbelt and then sitting beside me. He took my hand.

"You don't have to hold my hand," I said.

"Yes, but I want to," he replied, squeezing my hand and holding it tight. He smiled at me. Past his shoulder, out the window, I saw the lights of Las Vegas. The city laid out like a brilliant patchwork blanket in the middle of the desert. The sun was rising in the east, casting a warm glow over everything.

The plane touched down, and we walked through the bustling airport to a waiting car. It wasn't just any car. It was Priscilla. My 1968 Pontiac Firebird. She was even more beautiful in the Las Vegas lights. The city reflected off her white paint like she was part of the city. Like she was Las Vegas.

"How did you get here?" I asked her as I ran my hand across her beautiful hood.

"I had her shipped here. Your mechanic is excellent," Matthew said from over my shoulder.

"Brian. I need to pay him."

"I took care of it."

"Thank you. Brian is a good man."

I slid into the driver's seat and took a moment to commune with my car. To apologize for crashing her into a gazebo and for leaving her so long. Then I turned the key and her engine roared to life. The rumble of her exhaust and the smell of oil and gasoline brought up memories of open roads. We had seen many years together.

Matthew and Thor got in and discussed business as I drove us through the city to the Strip. I ignored their muttering and focused on the sounds and the lights. My senses had slept for four years and now felt raw and open like a new wound under the glare of the lights and the pounding of the music. A few buildings had changed, but the city stayed the same; the rush and the sense of urgency, like a hummingbird flapping its wings so fast, it straddled life and death every second. The beat of the nightclubs like the heart of the city, pounding all day and all night.

When I pulled up to the Red Oasis, it looked the same too. But what was four years to a building of brick and steel? The lights flashed and spun like a bird displaying its colourful plumage. I drove into the dark of the underground garage and parked beside Matthew's reserved parking space, occupied by a Corolla. I laughed.

It was a blue one now. I supposed if he was going to drive a Corolla, at least he wasn't driving an old one.

"What's so funny?" Matthew asked.

"Your car choice."

"Some things change and still stay the same," he said. His words struck me silent.

I turned off the engine and ran my hand over the dashboard. Priscilla stayed the same.

We got out and took the elevator to the lobby. They had remodeled it since I was last here. The counter had a sleeker, modern, frosted glass top and all the shops had matching frosted glass frames around their display windows. There were more lights and the new design had a more spacious feel.

"I have some work to catch up on, but I'll come get you tonight and take you out. You should dine again." I nodded, and he handed me a key card.

"I kept your room for you. Your clothes are there or you can pick out some new clothes in the boutique if you like," he said before he kissed my cheek and turned away. He and Thor disappeared down the back halls.

An uncomfortable feeling settled in my stomach. Was I going to live here and spend Matthew's money? He had a lot, but it didn't feel right. I pushed the thought aside for now. I had cooled considerably over the last 24 hours and knew just the place to get warmed up.

TWENTY-THREE

The sauna was perfect. There were several people lounging around inside, but they spoke in hushed whispers and the room was hot as hell. I sighed and leaned back against the wall. My skin flushed as the heat permeated my bones. I stayed in there for an hour, listening to the quiet conversation of the humans. Getting little glimpses of their lives like a snapshot; there and then gone.

When I walked back out a young man stood from a bench. He was tall and broad. It wasn't until my eyes got to his face that I recognized him. Ben's hair was cut shorter. He had grown into his lanky body and his face had filled so his square jaw and high cheekbones made him handsome instead of gawky.

"Whoa, Ben. You're hot," I said with a wink.

He looked down, his cheeks going pink. I noticed the scar on his neck where the vampires who kidnapped him ripped him open.

"What are you doing here?" I asked.

He took out a small device, the size of a phone and typed into it like he was texting, but when he looked up again, the small device spoke for him in a masculine voice. "I live here. Matthew put me through college and gave me a job on his IT security team when I graduated last spring."

"That's great," I said.

Ben typed again.

"I'm glad Matthew could rescue you the way you rescued me," the electronic voice chirped.

I looked away.

"Sure. Listen, I have to get going, but I'll see you around, ok?"

Ben stared at me for a minute and then nodded.

I walked through the lobby to the door that led to the back halls, then through the halls to Matthew's office. I knocked and walked in. Remembering the last time I did that. When I saw him smiling at the blonde.

I shut the door behind me and Matthew looked up, his eyes sliding over my body, and I realized I was still in a swimsuit.

"What is wrong with me?"

"Is that a rhetorical question?" he replied.

"No, there is something wrong with me."

He stood up looking concerned. "They starved you for four years, I don't imagine everything will be as it was right away."

He didn't understand and I couldn't explain it. "You are probably right," I said and turned to go, but he took my hand and stopped me.

"You can tell me anything, you know. If you want to talk about what happened to you or anything else, I will always be here."

I bit my lip and nodded. He let me go, and I walked back out of his office.

I went up to my room and got dressed, then back down and out of the building. I followed the sidewalk, letting my feet walk me in whatever direction they wanted to go. This unsettled feeling was eating at me.

I found myself in front of the small white chapel, so I went inside. Hopefully, Father Elvis would have something to say.

When I walked in, the place was empty. It was the first time no one was around. I sat down in one of the tiny pews and waited.

Several minutes later, Father Elvis came out of a back room, buckling up his pants. His hair was grayer and his face was more lined. A brunette in a short skirt followed behind him, popping gum into her mouth. He saw me and stopped, and the brunette just walked past him and out the front door like I wasn't even there.

"Jesus, Ren. I thought you had left the city. What can I do for you?" he asked straightening his shirt.

I chuckled and shook my head. "Nothing." I stood to leave but then turned back. "Do you think a person can change?"

He paused for a moment. "If you are in old habits, set in your old ways, changes are a coming, for these are changing days," he sang the words with a western twang.

I nodded and walked back out of the chapel.

As the sun hid its eyes from the sins of the night, the people spilled out onto the streets. The music got louder as the crowds got thicker. Tourists with cameras were trying to take pictures of the night scenes. Evangelicals on the street corners, screaming about the good Lord. Homeless people settling down on cardboard boxes in back alleys. Drug dealers sitting on darkened street corners and passing out their wares to anyone with money.

Club Vein was busy. I wasn't wearing the best clothes for clubbing, but I went in anyway. It was early for hunting, so I ordered a drink and sat at the bar.

"This seat taken?" I looked beside me to see Matthew's smiling face. I smiled back as he sat down and ordered a drink. "You weren't in your room." "Had things to do," I said.

Matthew looked like he wanted to ask what I was up to, but held back. The DJ set up and began playing music as Matthew and I sat there.

"You took care of Ben," I said

"Yeah, I figured if you saved him, he was worth saving," he said.

"I didn't save him," I muttered.

"What?"

"I said I didn't save him. I was using his laptop. Err, I wanted to use his laptop. It has a password, I wanted…Never mind." I spoke so fast I wasn't sure if Matthew understood what I was saying.

Matthew turned in his bar stool so he was facing me. Then he studied me for a moment.

I kept my eyes on my glass, using my thumb to wipe the condensation from the outside.

"Thank you," he said. Then he took my hand and pulled me onto the dance floor. It was still empty, but Matthew tugged me into his arms and held me tight, moving me to the music. We danced for a long time, until the club filled with people and the heat of their bodies warmed the whole place. The smell of liquor and humanity tickled my nose and my teeth ached.

I scanned the room, looking for someone to hunt. Matthew moved his face in front of mine. He opened his mouth in a silent hiss, flashing his fangs at me, and then let me go and backed away until he had disappeared in the crowd like it was a wave taking him under.

I stood shocked for a minute until the hairs on the back of my neck rose and I spun around. It reminded me of the night they took me, but I shoved that thought away. Matthew was here. Now. I knew it was his eyes tracking me. The rush I felt was like the highest high. I danced with a pretty boy as a hunter hunted me.

When I hadn't felt him stalking me for a while, I moved across to the bar and ordered a drink. Then I felt him again. I spun to look for him, but he was invisible on the crowd. I sat on the bar stool and scanned the room. I thought I might have seen his head for a second by the DJ. I finished my drink and danced through the humans towards the front of the stage. When I got there, I couldn't see him, but felt his eyes on my back. This time I didn't turn around. I started dancing with a skinny punk kid. His hair was shaved into a short pink mohawk and the chains around his neck clinked, reminding me of being chained up in the basement.

I moved away from him and the memory he brought until I was next to a big muscular man. He turned and wrapped his thick arms around me and we danced while Matthew's eyes burned into my neck. I felt a cool breath on the back of my neck as his presence overwhelmed me. He hissed and the muscular guy dropped his hands from my hips like I had burned him.

I laughed and leaned back into Matthew's cool chest. His hands slid on to my hips and he pulled me flush against him as we moved to the beat in the middle of the sea of people. His mouth was at my ear until it slid down to my neck towards my collarbone. I tipped my head sideways and shivered. His cool lips traced the length of my neck, but his swaying body never lost the rhythm of the music. Finally, his hand came up and pointed to a leggy blonde. He definitely had a type.

He let me go, and I danced towards her. Then I turned in front of her and took her hand. She smiled at me and kept dancing. I moved in so our bodies were touching. She smelled like cinnamon candy hearts. Matthew's moved in behind her and I held his eyes over her shoulder, giving him a smirk. When the music switched to a new song, I bared my fangs at the young woman. Her eyes went wide, and she tipped her head in invitation. Matthew turned her body so he could keep eye contact with me and latched onto her neck. His arms wrapped around her as her eyes rolled up in her head.

Matthew drank his fill, his eyes never leaving mine and let her go. She teetered for a second and caught her balance, then wandered towards the bar.

Matthew took me back in his arms and sealed his mouth to mine. He smelled like candy and tasted delicious, making my teeth ache even more. I wanted to go find my dinner, but when I pulled away, he held tighter and tipped his head.

I stared into his eyes for a moment, unsure if he was serious. His smile was like the sun shining on a hot summer morning.

I leaned in and licked his neck and his hand slid into my hair, cradling the back of my head. The moan that left my throat was cut off by the tang of his blood as it slid into my mouth like syrup. My heart sputtered and then pounded louder than the baseline of the music in the club, drowning out the sounds around me. Just his heart and mine, nothing else. I expected his knees to give out, but instead, he swayed to our rhythm, and when I had drunk my fill, I pulled my teeth from his neck and let a drop appear on the surface of his skin as his body healed. The strobe lights from above reflected off the shiny drop of blood before I licked it. Then I threw my head back and let Matthew move me like I was a rag doll. His heart and mine, beating together. Thump. Thump. Thump. Totally attuned. Just us two.

The night went on and on and when we left the club, we went home together.

TWENTY-FOUR

"I'd like you to talk to Emily again," Matthew said the next day in his office. I had been flipping through a medical book. I found it funny that Matthew had learned to heal humans. He was an MD who ran a casino. If any old people who came to gamble had a heart attack when they lost all their money, he could save their lives.

"Why?" I asked. I knew why I wanted him to say it out loud.

"Because she can help you. You've been through a lot and I think you have things you need to talk about."

"Emily is afraid of me," I said, dropping my eyes back to the photo of all the veins in a human body.
They had a ton of veins.

"What have you done to dissuade her fear of you?"

He had a point. But did I want her to not be afraid of me? What purpose did that serve?

"She's obsessed with you and my father," I complained.

"Is she? Or did she want you to talk about me and your father?"

I didn't reply. I flipped the page and looked at the anatomy chart on the next page. Naked man pictures trumped nagging psychiatrist boyfriends. Did I call him my boyfriend? Yeah, let's pretend I didn't.

———

November 30th, 1963

The sixties were a haven for vampires. Everyone was high, and we took them higher.

"No, man. Hydrogen bombs. They will wipe out the whole world, man."

"Nothing lasts forever," Walt replied, coolly.

Walt was a vampire, but, at the time, I thought he had no dreams of climbing the vampire hierarchy. He was a rebel, and we fed off each other, figuratively. And sometimes literally.

"There is no life after death. We will all be dead." The stoners were such philosophers.

"Maybe you will be, but I plan to live forever," Walt replied, turning and flashing me his fangs where the silly humans couldn't see.

I laughed and leaned back in my seat. Walt and I hitched a ride in the little Volkswagen bus with five humans who were crossing the country. It was cramped and uncomfortable most of the time, but they were going our way and they were delicious. At night they would set up tents and camp along the side of the road or at a music concert. We had already been travelling a week but had only made it from Texas to the Mississippi. It was a very interesting time to be alive. The counterculture suited me and my interests. People drifted and paused often. We could walk up to anyone with a spare seat in their vehicle and they would welcome us along, but it was still before the coming out, so the fact they were all stoned covered our tracks.

The man finally passed out, leaving Walt and I to ourselves. The silence stretched on for a minute and then Walt spoke again. "I have to tell you something, Nia."

"What is it?" I laughed, assuming his serious tone was a joke.

"It's serious." He looked back at me and his face matched his tone for once.

"What?"

"I've done something. I thought they would protect me, but I think they've thrown me under the bus."

Walt's eyes had no twinkle of mischief. I studied his face, trying to decide if I wanted to know or not.

"Just know, I did what they told me to do. I didn't want to, but…" He reached over and tucked a strand of my hair behind my ear.

"But what?" I asked cautiously.

"It's nothing. The paranoid humans are probably rubbing off on me." He smoothed back his long hair and shook off the serious mask, but a feeling of dread settled in my stomach.

The next morning, the hippies gathered themselves up and drove us on past the Mississippi River and just kept going right into Alabama. The further we drove, the more Walt seemed to calm down. His twinkle returned, but sometimes I caught him repeatedly glancing out the back window like he thought we were being followed. I saw nothing.

Just outside Tuscaloosa, we pulled off into a quiet park and the hippies wandered into the forest. They liked the forest, but Walt and I would often have to go track them down if they were gone too long. They would pass out in a group and then wake up and do more drugs. Walt and I lay in the back of the bus, relaxing. I was trying to get some sleep, but Walt was tossing and turning. I put my hand on his chest to stop him, he sighed and stilled.

The screech of tires, cut through the silence and Walt shot up like something had bitten him. He crawled to the front of the bus and out the door.

I went after him but was stopped at the door by a solid body.

"Lavinia, what are you doing running with the likes of this man?"

"Father," I breathed. "How did you find me?"

"I always know where you are Lavinia, but I am not here for you, only your companion."

I heard a yell and pushed past my father. Two men in red coats and black tactical gear had pinned Walt to the ground.

"It was all for you Nia!" Walt called, though one of the men squeezed his neck so he could say no more.

One of the Blood Guard pulled out a stake.

"No!" I attempted to run towards him, but my father's steel arms wrapped around me. Pinning my arms to my side and lifting my feet off the ground.

"Stop, Lavinia or they will think you were part of his crime," my father said into my hair.

"Whatever it is, he is innocent!" I yelled, still struggling against my fathers hold.

"He killed the president, Nia," my father said.

Walt's eyes caught mine from between the legs of the Blood Guard and he mouthed the words 'I'm sorry'.

"It's a mistake! He wouldn't do that!"

A bloody tear ran from Walt's eye towards the grass as the Blood Guard drove the stake through his heart. The light went out from his eyes as the tear disappeared in the grass.

My father let me go, and I collapsed.

That was the end of Walt.

I never found out why he did what he did. But vampires came out of the closet soon after and the presidential replacement, Johnson, was awfully welcoming of our kind.

———

Present

I closed the medical book and took it back to the shelf. I tipped my head to read the spines of the other books, but, I couldn't focus on the titles, considering Matthew and whether he was my boyfriend. Seemed like a stupid title anyway. Nobody used such an immature phrase to describe someone anymore. They used partner or significant other or lover. I liked lover. It sounded fun. A lot less serious, anyway.

That settled, I refocused my eyes on the book titles only to realize Matthew had left his chair and was standing right beside me. I straightened and picked a book at random.

"Excellent choice."

I read the book cover. 'Abnormal Psychology'. "Shit," I said, returning the book to the shelf.

"Why are you so opposed to having someone to talk to? Your Officer Jenkins told me you used to go to confession. It's the same thing."

"He told you that? I will rip his eyebrow off."

Matthew laughed, but I was serious. Jenkins better not be blabbing about me to anyone who passes by.

"I tried going to confession here, it wasn't the same." I flopped down on the chair in the corner. Matthew leaned on the bookcase and crossed one ankle over the other. He looked dashing and pensive standing like that. We were silent for a long time. I didn't know what Matthew was thinking, but I was trying to decide what I wanted to do with my life. I needed something that was my own. Something worthwhile.

"I want a job," I said, pulling Matthew out of his thoughts.

"You want to deal cards?"

"I guess, for now. I need to do something other than what I've always done."

"That sounds like a good plan. A healthy plan. I would still like you to talk to someone."

I stood up and strode towards the door. "Can you ask Carson to get me a shift today?" I asked and then walked out the door and headed for my suite to find my work clothes. Hopefully, they weren't still balled up in a corner somewhere.

———

That day I worked a busy blackjack table. Dealing cards and taking chips. I wasn't sure how anyone made money at blackjack considering I was taking way more coins than anyone else, but everyone seemed to enjoy losing their money.

Halfway through my shift, a sound was niggling at the edge of my hearing. I was sliding cards from the shuffling machine to waiting gamblers, I could do that in my sleep, but somewhere on the casino floor, there was a sound.

It was a drip.

No, a heartbeat.

Thump. Thump.

I scanned the casino floor between deals, trying to pinpoint the location of the sound. It wasn't the heartbeat of the people around me. At least none within view. This was different.

I dealt another hand. Thor appeared beside me so I must have messed up, but I hadn't noticed. I gave him a smile and dealt another hand. The sound didn't stop though. That steady heartbeat pumping blood around a warm body. A vein bulging in delight. Throbbing to the beat of the drum inside the chest. Bloody saliva filled my mouth, and I tried to focus on the card game so Thor would leave. The heart was mine. I didn't want Thor to have it. The humans all around me had soft heartbeats, but I didn't want their hearts.

I wanted that beautiful heart, singing a song for only my ears.

Mine.

As my shift wore on, the sound was like music, forcing my movements. I moved to its beat and longed for its warm embrace.

Carson stopped at my table with another dealer to let me know my shift was over. The man in a uniform just like mine took my place at the table and dealt cards. Carson asked me to meet him in the break room in a few minutes, so I stopped at the bar and got a drink.

That's when I heart the heart, so close I could touch it. My teeth throbbed with longing. It was behind the bar, but when I leaned over the counter, I realized it wasn't a heart at all. It was the beer tap, dripping into the tray below. Drip. Drip.

I laughed at my own foolish imagination. The boredom of dealing cards was definitely more than my mind could handle. I would need to find something more interesting to do. I wove through the slot machines towards the break room. The sounds of coins and music overloaded my hearing.

I went through the door and the sounds faded as the door swung closed behind me. I sat down at a small table with my drink. Carson came in a moment later.

"So, how was your first shift back?" he asked, sliding into the seat across from me. He didn't do small talk, so I narrowed my eyes at him.

He chuckled and scratched his neck. "All right, what are you doing?"

"I'm having a drink with you," I said, holding up my glass.

"No, in the casino. We both know you could do anything and you don't need the money."

"I don't know what I want to do, Carson."

"Well you better figure it out, if you are still working in this casino in a year, I will kick your ass." He smiled and then got up and walked to the door.

"Good talk!" I called after him.

I walked through the casino floor, towards the elevator in the lobby.

"Hey, Nia," an electronic voice said from behind me. I spun around to see Ben standing by the door to the casino with his text to talk device.

"Oh, hey, Ben. How's it going?"

He typed for a moment and then looked up as the voice started again. "I would like to talk to you if you have time," it said.

"Sure, how about tonight though? Around 8? I'm tired right now."

He typed out a message. "Ok, I'll meet you upstairs.

My room is on your floor."

"Super, see ya then," I replied.

I took the elevator back up to my suite. Matthew had given me a key card to his suite, but he was working and I felt more comfortable in mine. I curled up on the couch and turned on the TV.

Carson was right, I needed to find something more to do than dealing cards. I had a degree in business and another in art history. Neither gave me a career, but they were an easy and fun way to pass the time. I could go back to school. What was four more years?

I had driven past the University of Nevada. It wasn't too far from the casino. I could go in the morning and see what courses were offered.

I was uncomfortable on the couch so I moved to the bed and curled into a ball. The tap in the bathroom broke the silence. The drip had returned. I would have to call Henry in the morning if he still worked here. Remembering Henry's face when he showed up at my suite to fix the tap last time and I scared him made me laugh. I bet I could pull it off again. Henry was a nervous type.

I lay for a long time, listening to the heartbeat before I fell asleep.

TWENTY-FIVE

The heart kept beating. I couldn't move or see, but the heart was right in front of me.

"Come closer," I whispered to the heart. It had to come closer.

It kept beating or was it dripping? No, it was beating. Right there.

I counted out its rhythm. Thump. Thump.

I was so hungry. I just wanted a taste. I strained, trying to move. If I could just move a bit further.

"Come closer," I begged.

My finger twitched, I felt it move. I was sure. I twitched it again. And then my hand. My whole arm moved across the hard surface.

Thump.

Thump.

The heart was beating faster and louder. I moved my leg and then slid off the surface. I was moving. Going to find the heart and drink.

Finally.

I followed the sound across the room. There was a door, and I reached for it. The heart was on the other side. Beating just for me.

I gripped the doorknob, ready to pounce. The thumping was louder, drowning out everything else. The world narrowed down to only me and the heart. It pushed blood through veins like chocolate syrup through a straw.

I turned the doorknob and swung open the door at the same moment as I pounced. It wouldn't escape this time. It had been teasing me for so long. My prey, just out of reach, but not anymore.

My teeth sunk home and pulled the first delicious mouthful. The prey tried to pull back, but I held on tight and pulled another swallow of life into my body. The taste was like nothing I had ever had. I was so hungry, I kept pulling until my prey subsided and collapsed into my arms. My pliant donor. My precious heart. As I continued to swallow, I wondered if it would ever end. Would the heart keep beating forever? Would it bring me back to life? Would it fill me until I burst?

The moment stretched on as the heartbeat slowed. And then the most dramatic final beat rung through my ears as I released the heart and felt my own chest shake with a resounding thump.

My body could hardly contain it. The beat was strong and vibrant and pulsed hard enough I could feel it like an entire marching band inside my chest. I put my hand over it and savoured the moment. The beautiful life that lived inside me. It was perfect.

I looked down at the heartbeat finally, but it wasn't a heartbeat.

It was a man.

It was Ben.

And he was dead.

TWENTY-SIX

Things moved quickly after that. My heart beat a staccato as security guards and Matthew raced off the elevator. Too late to save him. Too late to save me.

I covered my mouth, like that could take back what I had just done.

"It was the heart. It was…" I realized how foolish that sounded.

"What have you done?" Matthew asked. "What have you done!" He repeated, much louder.

"I've drunk from the heart," I said, still unsure if I was awake or asleep.

"How could you do this?" Matthew asked, stepping over Ben's lifeless form.

"I thought he was the heart," I said, but it made little sense to me either.

"What heart?" Matthew yelled the question like he could get me to make sense if only he spoke loud enough. Bloody tears sprung to my eyes like I had any right to cry when I had stolen a life.

"Sir, do you want me to call the Blood Guard?"

"Nobody is doing anything," he said over his shoulder before turning back. "Tell me what happened?" Matthew grabbed my shoulders and his fingers dug in painfully. I deserved the pain. I deserved much worse. The gravity of what I had done was setting in. It was a line I had never crossed.

"I killed Ben."

"No!" Matthew yelled. He turned to Thor, "You didn't see anything! Someone clean up the mess!"

"You can't hide this, Matthew," I pleaded. "If the Blood Guard find out, they will kill you too."

"These people work for me! I am Lord of this city!" he roared. The men around him bowed their heads and averted their eyes. Even if they were loyal, word would get out. Someone with aspirations of having a city would tell the Blood Guard and they would find the evidence they needed. This whole building was monitored 24/7. There were vampires watching us on TV monitors right now. There, on the ceiling outside my door was a plastic dome. I looked at its blinking eye in the center. Watching, judging.

Matthew followed my line of sight and a sound of anger and despair churned from his throat as he slammed his palms to his forehead.

"You know it won't work. Matthew, please?" I begged.

Matthew put a hand on either side of my face and searched my eyes for the answer he longed for, but it wasn't there. There was no solution to this problem.

"Please, don't call my father. My poor mother's heart would break." Then I pressed my hand to his chest. "You have to do it."

"I can't."

"Please! Matthew. I killed Ben. He is dead." I collapsed to the ground and rested my head in my hands. Ben had a whole life ahead of him. I had robbed him of the one thing I longed for. The one thing I could never have. I reached out and took his hand in mine. It was still warm, but wouldn't be for long.

"Sir," Thor said from behind Matthew.

When he didn't respond I looked up to find Matthew's face a mask of grief and sorrow.

Thor looked down at me with sadness, but he had a stake in his hand.

"Please Thor? Don't let my father come. I can't bear to have his face be the last I see on this earth." My words choked out.

"No, Nia. Call the king," Matthew ordered sealing my fate. My father would look down on me with disgust. He would be the one to command them to kill me. His face would be the last I saw.

"Please, Nia. Let me talk to him. Let me do this for you." He crouched in front of me. Brushing my hair back for my face, but all I could do was stare at Ben. At what I had destroyed.

Matthew spoke to his men for a moment before scooping me up off the floor. He carried me away from Ben's cooling body. Setting me down on the bed, he flicked on the heated blanket. I didn't deserve comfort. I didn't deserve Matthew's body stretched out beside me, or his gentle fingers smoothing my hair.

I deserved the darkness. The pain and nothingness.

"Tell me what happened," he whispered.

I swallowed, refusing the tears. "I heard the heart. Do you hear it?" The bathroom taps. Drip.

"I don't understand," he said.

I laughed, but there was no humour to it. "Because it makes no sense. There was a drip. In the dungeon, I lived in. It was a heart. I heard it beat. I called to it and it called back."

Matthew lay back on the bed beside me and stared at the ceiling, considering my words.

"It wasn't your fault."

"It's never my fault, is it?"

"What?"

"Nothing."

————

Fall 1971

We had just outed ourselves to the world and there was a growing movement that supported our rights. Mostly because we were wealthy and held various positions of authority. Father had entered politics a decade ago and moved his way up so he was in a prime position. I was sure he had orchestrated the entire thing. He was meticulous, and the day we came out to the world, we weren't just welcomed, they worshipped us.

The president was already a disciple.

"Today is a good day for America and the world," President Nixon droned on, making the absurd normal. That was my father's genius.

"We welcome these people, who have lived peacefully among us all this time, into our society. My fellow Americans, join me in welcoming to the stage, the king of the vampires, King Garth."

The crowd gathered at the white house clapped and cheered and acted as though the monster before them was a saviour. His very presence was proof that life existed beyond their imagination. He embodied the magic they wanted to believe in. I puked in my mouth a little.

I turned away from the TV in the window of the electronics store and continued down the street towards my favourite bar. It was full of old tired working-class people. They suited me at the time. Everyday people who struggled to stay alive and drank to forget about it. I dined on people who passed out behind the bar at closing time. I had no joy. It died with Walt.

One night I went behind the bar to see who hadn't made it home and found a man standing over the body of a young woman. He looked up at me and the street light shone on his face. I would later learn his name, but on this night, I turned on my heel and walked away. It was 2 years and a dozen more bodies before they caught him.

I always wondered if draining that serial killer might have saved my soul.

The following morning, the Blood Guard escorted me through the casino. Matthew was hot on our heels. They had taken Ben away, removing all trace of him. The scent of blood no longer hung in the air.

"Don't worry, Nia. I'll be in the car right behind you."

Poor Matthew. Tragedy struck anyone who happened to get too close to me. I was cursed from the day of my birth. When I came screaming into the world, they should have just hit me over the head with a rock.

They escorted me to the back seat of an SUV. The tinted windows hid the fact that it was reinforced inside with heavy steel. The vehicle was made for transporting vampires.

I curled up on the seat and slept my way across the country. I dreaded seeing my father's face. His stern eyes, his scowling mouth twisted in rage. He would not forgive me this. He was most likely selecting his new heir now. A king must have an heir.

They pulled me from the back seat in the gated front yard of my father's home. He had moved to Beverly Hills when he retired from politics and took over his kingly duties.

Matthew sat in his car just beyond the gate. It seemed they would not let him in. He looked like he wanted to tear down the fence, but we both knew what would happen. Father could easily replace Matthew with another keen vampire with high aspirations.

"Oh, my baby," my mother's voice rang through the air like a sweet bell. Tears welled in my eyes and I stumbled as I turned away from thoughts of Matthew and towards the person who had loved me with all my failings.

"Mummy," I whispered into her hair as she wrapped me up tight in her arms. I felt like a little girl again. Like the world would never reach me because I was safe in my mother's arms. Sobs shook her body.

"What have you done?" she whispered over and over, but I couldn't answer her. I had broken her heart. That was what I had done. The final piece of my downfall was knowing I had done what I had thought impossible. I ruined the one last good thing I had in life.

The Blood Guard pulled me from her arms. Momma put her hand on my cheek. Her face a ruin of sadness. A look I never thought I would see from her.

The Blood Guard turned me towards the door where my father stood. His stern face was as I imagined it would be. He suffered me for the sake of my mother. Now I had broken my mother.

He turned and strode back into the house. They led me to follow him through the front door and down the halls of the cold mansion to his study. I knew the place. I had been here a decade ago. When he tried to convince me to be what he wanted the last time.

———

10 years earlier.

"Lavinia, you cannot go on like this. You must step up and take this city. I have asked nothing of you your whole life."

I scoffed at my father's words.

"Let one of your devoted followers have the city," I replied.

"This is ridiculous. I'm offering you the best city in all the country, probably the world. You don't even have to do anything. Let your subordinates take care of it, just be the figurehead."

I turned to leave. It was all a ploy. He would run my life if I had a city. If I stepped into public life, I would be under his thumb forever. "Stop!" he commanded.

"I came to see mother. Why can't you accept that I don't want this?"

"You have responsibilities, Lavinia!"

I walked out of his office. My mother stood by the front door, clutching my jacket to her chest like it was a baby. I was a grown up though, no longer a child she could cradle in her arms.

"Sorry," I muttered. I hated putting her in between us.

"I love you, Nia. He does too. In his way."

I gave her a sad smile.

"I love you too, momma."

———

Present.

"Thank you, you may go," he said to the Blood Guard.

"Why am I here?" I asked.

"I wanted to give you one last chance. Step up now, become a leader and I will not let this news travel any further. You can live."

"I killed a boy."

"He doesn't matter," my father replied, sitting down at his desk. His face gave him away. He thought he finally had me. He thought he could control me now that I had done this thing.

"No."

He looked up. "Then you will die."

"Then I will die."

He slammed his hands down on his desk. Papers flew. I flinched.

"That is not an option!" He yelled.

"Why not? I will never live up to your expectations, father!" Stepping forward, his eyes burned into mine. "I will never be the one you want! Just choose another heir and move on with your life."

"You selfish child! Your mother will not abide by your death!"

"You mean, she won't forgive you." I laughed cruelly. I don't know why I hadn't thought of that sooner. Of course, she wouldn't. I was what kept them together, like some sad little band-aid on their relationship.

"Guard," he called. "You will have some time to think about it. A decade should help change your mind."

"No, father, don't," The guard came in and grabbed my arms. "Please, papa!" I begged. I couldn't go through that again. The guard wrestled me past my crying mother and into the basement of my father's mansion. "One hundred years won't make a difference! You can't do this! Please! Just kill me now!" I screamed. The whole city could have heard me.

Locked in my cell, I looked around for anything I could use to kill myself. There was not a single scrap of wood in the room. It would be days before I seized up. The room was warm, and I had eaten the day before. Poor Ben.

I yelled and banged on the bars for hours, but no one came. When I kicked and raged at the walls, they didn't budge. The stone was thick and solid. It wasn't a newer cinder block basement. It was an old crawl space. The house above did not indicate that it had any history at all. It was polished and modern when I walked through, but this space told a different story.

And as my body cooled over the following days, I lay on my back. I tried to tell myself it wouldn't be so bad. I had done it once, I could do it again. Ten years. Maybe then he would kill me when I refused to live under his thumb.

After some time, my limbs stopped moving. I lost sensation and sense of time passing. There was no drip here. Only silence. I filled it with thoughts. My mind spun through all the moments with Matthew. I tried to keep the look on his face when I disappointed him from my memory, but it kept creeping in. Then my mother's face. I was the root of all evil.

My eyes closed for the last time. I tried to force them open later when I heard a noise. It was too late for that though. I listened. A footstep. A slide of a shoe on the floor. The jingle of a key turning in a lock.

A breath as the door slid open on silent hinges.

A gasp as whoever it was laid eyes on my form. It must have been months by now. I probably looked like a shriveled monster.

The bed squeaked as someone sat beside me.

"Hello, Nia."

I would have cried at the sound of Matthew's voice if I still had the ability to move. He had come to save me from my tragic condition.

"I had hoped you could still see," he said.

I heard another rustle and then felt hot blood splash on my tongue. The pain was less intense this time, but he still had to stifle my voice when the warmth hit my cold body.

"I'm sorry," he whispered. A bloody tear traced the side of my face.

"Help... me." I stuttered through my tight jaw. He bit his lip and nodded. He knew what I needed. Not a knight in shining armor, this time. I needed an angel of mercy today.

"I will," Matthew said, wiping a tear from his face.

Matthew lay down beside me. Our legs intertwined like branches in a hurricane. Holding on for dear life.

He tucked my hair behind my ear and ran his fingers across my cheek, his eyes still flicking around, absorbing my features.

I felt the approaching peace of oblivion. The peace I could never find while I was alive. It was right there, moving over me like the rising of the sea. I looked into Matthew's sky-blue eyes. I was wrong, I didn't prefer green eyes, I loved the sky on a summer day. The peaceful lake just after sunrise as the loon calls. I loved the blue eyes of the man who wouldn't let me go.

"I love you, Nia," he whispered.

When I looked away, he moved my chin back, so I was looking him in the eye again.

"Doubt thou the stars are fire, doubt that the sun doth move." A sob shook his body and fresh tears blinded me as he continued. "Doubt truth to be a liar," he paused and took a shaky breath. "But never doubt I love."

I bit my lip and tried to compose myself. I had one more thing to say to him. As he raised the stake above my pounding heart, I took a deep breath and whispered, "For in that sleep of death, what dreams may come."

The end.